This was ridicu

Holly only had to
didn't have to like
Sam Stratton tha
irrationally edgy? She had spent the two years
since Martin's death trying to pick up the
pieces, and was just beginning to get her life
into some sort of order. She didn't need Sam's
particular brand of arrogance; she didn't need
the kind of disruption she just knew he was
going to cause. Working with the man was
easy—she could still maintain a distance—but
having him as a neighbour? Now that was
quite a different kettle of fish!

Jean Evans was born in Leicester and married shortly before her seventeenth birthday. She has two married daughters and several grandchildren. She gains valuable information and background for her medical romances from her husband, who is a senior nursing administrator. She now lives in Hampshire, close to the New Forest, and within easy reach of the historic city of Winchester.

Recent titles by the same author:

HEART ON THE LINE
THE FRAGILE HEART
A DANGEROUS DIAGNOSIS
NO LEASE ON LOVE

A PRACTICE MADE PERFECT

BY

JEAN EVANS

MILLS & BOON

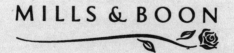

For Emma, Amy and Alexandra,
with love

MILLS & BOON, the Rose Device and LOVE ON CALL are trademarks of the publisher.
Harlequin Mills & Boon Limited,
Eton House, 18–24 Paradise Road, Richmond, Surrey TW9 1SR
This edition published by arrangement with
Harlequin Enterprises B.V.

© Jean Evans 1995

ISBN 0 263 79093 2

Set in 10 on 11 pt Linotron Times
03-9506-58099

Typeset in Great Britain by CentraCet, Cambridge
Made and printed in Great Britain

CHAPTER ONE

IT HAD begun to rain earlier in the day. Gradually, as the December afternoon wore on, the rain had turned to snow; light, feathery flakes at first, driven by an increasingly bitter wind.

Dr Holly Palmer glanced anxiously at the leaden sky and shivered. 'It looks pretty awful out there. Are you sure you won't at least stay and have some coffee?'

Her sandy-haired companion shook his head, smiling ruefully. 'I'm tempted, but I'd better get started if I'm going to make it back to Birmingham tonight.' He glanced at his watch and shrugged himself into his coat, turning up the collar. 'If I make a dash for it I should just about catch the three-thirty train.' He held out his hand. 'It's been nice meeting you.'

'Thank you for coming, Dr Forbes.' Holly shook the proffered hand, a smile curving her generous mouth. 'Obviously Dr Wainwright and I need to chat, but I promise I'll telephone and leave a message, if necessary, as soon as we've made our final decision.'

'I appreciate it.'

'I'm sure you have nothing to worry about. Have a safe journey.' She grinned. 'And don't let the weather put you off. It's lovely up here in the spring.'

She watched him disappear into the gathering gloom of a Yorkshire afternoon, shivering again as a flurry of snow wafted into the waiting-room, ruffling her dark chestnut hair. She was still smiling as she closed the door. She had taken a liking to Graham Forbes. He was young, enthusiastic, easy to get on with. The sort

5

that, if the practice had to have a locum, she would be happy to work with.

The rustling of a newspaper brought her up with a start and, for several seconds, she found herself staring into thickly-lashed, disturbingly blue eyes which at that moment were filled with a sardonic amusement that made her pulses quicken even as her own blue eyes flashed her annoyance. For a moment there she had completely forgotten the other short-listed candidate. Her cheeks flushed.

'I'm sorry you've been kept waiting, Dr Stratton. It shouldn't be for too much longer. Is someone looking after you?' She glanced at the tray with its empty cup. 'Would you like some more coffee?'

The newspaper was lowered, riveting her attention on the man who rose slowly to his feet. She felt as if an electric current had passed through her body. It wasn't just the overwhelming sense of self-assurance which seemed to emanate from him as he stood there, though that in itself was sufficient to send a shiver of awareness running down her spine, it was something in the piercingly blue eyes which raked her slender figure and delicate features with an intensity so blatantly sexual that it almost took her breath away.

'I don't think so, thank you. I'll just await your decision, then be on my way, though thankfully not as far as Birmingham—tonight, at any rate.'

He folded the newspaper, setting it down on the table. He was tall, slim and muscular, and she was once again made immediately conscious of every line, from the taut shoulders to the slender waist and lean thighs beneath the dark trousers he was wearing.

With a determined effort she dragged her gaze up to meet his. 'Well, we certainly won't keep you waiting a moment longer than is absolutely necessary.'

'Take all the time you need.' His eyes narrowed, as

if to mock what he knew to be an air of assumed self-confidence. 'I'm quite happy to have the chance to sit and observe. You seem to have a very efficient system working here.'

Holly's mouth compressed as she nodded briefly. Arrogant—that was the word she had been looking for. She smiled stiffly. 'Yes, well, we do our best. Now, if you'll excuse me.' She hurried through to the consulting-room, where Uncle Matt was pouring coffee.

Proffering her a cup, he went to sit at the desk, tapping the stem of his empty pipe against the palm of his hand.

'Well, that all went well, don't you think?'

Holly smiled, spooning sugar into her coffee and helping herself to a biscuit. 'Yes, it did. In fact, it was surprisingly painless, once we'd whittled the list down to the final candidates. Oh, Graham—Dr Forbes—decided to get back, by the way. The weather's not too good. I said we'd phone him as soon as we'd come to a decision.'

'Well, that shouldn't take too long.' Matt Wainwright settled into his chair. 'I'd say the choice is pretty clear-cut.'

'I agree.' Shifting some papers, Holly sat on the edge of the desk, wrapping her hands round her cup. 'I'd say it's a straightforward choice. Dr Forbes is keen. He's young, I know, but he has a good manner and that counts for a lot. I think the patients would take to him. Yes——' she nodded '—I was impressed. As far as I'm concerned he'll make a welcome addition to the practice.'

Matthew Wainwright stared unhappily at the papers on his desk. 'My dear, I'm afraid we seem to be talking at cross-purposes.' He frowned. 'When I said the choice was clear-cut, I wasn't referring to Dr Forbes. I'm sorry. I can see you feel quite strongly about this, but I was referring to Dr Stratton.'

Holly stared at him. 'Stratton? But. . .I don't understand.'

'My dear, I agree. Dr Forbes is a nice young chap—young being the operative word.' He sucked at his unlit pipe, a habit of his when he was troubled. 'But the truth is, this practice needs someone with experience. By his own admission, Forbes is more or less straight out of medical school, apart from one other short spell as a locum. I'm sure he's a fine doctor, but I'm looking to ease your workload, not carry a second, albeit temporary partner while he finds his feet. Dr Stratton has experience. Three years in a large, inner-city teaching hospital, a year abroad and a year's surgical experience. That has to count for something.'

'I'm sure it does, but we're hardly what he's been used to,' Holly said caustically.

Matthew Wainwright fixed her with a troubled stare. 'I had a feeling you didn't exactly take to him.'

She rose to her feet, feeling slightly ashamed of her short temper. 'It isn't that, exactly.' That was the trouble. It was difficult to put her finger on one specific point. She shook herself mentally. What on earth was the matter with her? For the past two years she hadn't even noticed a man, much less looked at one, until suddenly Sam Stratton had come striding into the room, his presence stirring up a feeling of—of something she would rather not put into words.

She pushed a strand of hair behind her ear. 'Uncle Matt, I'm not complaining. You know how I feel about taking on a locum. I've managed so far. I can cope, at least until you feel well enough to get back to work.'

'I know——' Matt pressed a hand over hers '—and I appreciate what you've done. You don't complain, but you're doing more than your share and——'

'I can manage. The odd extra night call isn't any great hardship, and weekends aren't a problem. It's not as if I have any commitments. It's you I worry about.'

'Well, there's no need. My dear, it isn't fair to ask you to go on coping alone. I know. . .' He raised a hand, silencing her protest. 'You've done marvellously well, but the practice is expanding and there's a limit to how long you can go on carrying the workload alone.' He gave a wry smile which didn't quite reach his eyes. 'We need a locum, if only to ease my conscience, just until I'm back on my feet again.'

Holly looked at him keenly. 'The doctors said you need to convalesce. . .'

He waved the suggestion away. 'I never take any notice of what doctors say.'

'Uncle Matt, you had quite a severe heart attack. They're advising you for your own good.'

'Ach! I've heard it all before. I'm as fit as a fiddle, always was. I'm certainly not going to start acting like an invalid now. The sooner I get back to work the better. You know me, can't abide sitting around doing nothing.'

She joined in with his laughter, but wasn't fooled. Her glance flickered in his direction. The change in Matthew Wainwright over the recent weeks had shocked her, even though she was careful not to let it show as she looked at the once stout frame, now considerably thinner, and saw the tell-tale greyish tinge to his mouth. Her throat tightened.

'How long did they say before you're allowed back to work—officially, that is?' she added with a smile.

He sighed. 'They mentioned three months. Ridiculous, of course. They're playing safe and I told 'em so. Provided I take it easy, I see no reason why I can't potter around, do the odd spot of paperwork. In the meantime——' he sat back and studied her '—it isn't fair to ask you to cope alone. I know you would and I'm not doubting your abilities, but Sam Stratton is a good doctor. We're lucky to get him. He could have aimed for a bigger practice. . .'

'So why didn't he?'

'He explained, quite well, I thought, that he felt he needed a change. I can't say I blame the man.'

Holly stifled a sigh. Her uncle's arguments didn't dispel her doubts, but she managed to hide them, for his sake, and perhaps she was being unreasonable. 'You're right,' she smiled. 'I know it makes sense.' She gave a slight laugh. 'If I'm honest, it will be nice to have someone else to take a share of the night calls. I hate being hauled out of bed at three in the morning, especially this time of the year.'

'I don't think any of us ever quite get used to that.' There was a tiny but distinct note of relief in his voice as he laughed. 'So, you're happy then, about inviting Dr Stratton to join our practice?'

Holly gave him a reluctant smile. 'Of course. Take no notice of me. I'm just having a bad day, that's all.'

'Problems?'

She gave a short laugh. 'Nothing I can't handle. I got an urgent call to the Stibbings' place.'

'Not again.'

She nodded. 'Chest pains this time, according to the very brief message I got. I had to leave the car at the end of the lane. You know what it's like up there—it's just as well I carry a pair of boots with me. I waded through half a mile of mud and, when I finally got to the farm, Bill Stibbings was sitting at the kitchen table, large as life, enjoying a hearty breakfast and demanding to know if I'd brought his indigestion mixture with me. I wasn't too happy, I can tell you.'

Matt laughed. 'I can imagine. I hope you gave him a good talking-to?'

'Oh, I think the message got through. Not that I imagine for one minute it will stop him doing it again.' She grinned, then sobered. 'Anyway, this isn't solving the problem, is it?'

'I think it proves my point, that the sooner we take someone on, the sooner he can share the joys of the Bill Stibbingses of this world.'

Smiling, Holly leaned on the desk, her chin cupped in her hands, unaware that Matthew Wainwright was studying her intently and with some concern, seeing the pale features and the faint shadows beneath the thickly fringed eyes. Attractive rather than beautiful, Holly's delicate features were of the kind that would make anyone look twice at the slender young woman in the practical but modern dark trousers and silk shirt.

There was a look of sadness in the blue eyes. Not that it became apparent too often. It was only in moments of quiet reflection, as now, that he would catch a glimpse of something hidden in the quiet depths of her face.

'You're sure you have no practical objections to Dr Stratton?' His own eyes twinkled with mischief. 'Apart from the fact that he thought you were about eighteen and far too young to be a doctor. If so, I'm happy to listen,' he added gently.

Angry colour flared briefly in her cheeks then, with an effort, she smiled. 'No, really. I know you're right, and if it means I can persuade you to take things more easily. . .'

'My dear, I hope this is as much for you as it is for me. You can't go on like this.' He saw the faint tightening of his niece's mouth. 'Two years is a long time, you know. Why not give yourself a chance? Get out, meet people. I know you loved him, but Martin wasn't the only man in the world, you know.'

Holly stared at him bleakly. It was on the tip of her

tongue to say, But he was for me, and knew it would be useless. Stubbornly she tried to conjure up a picture of her husband. It was disconcerting to find that it was blurred, hazy, as it so often was these days. She blinked hard, shocked by the admission, and put it down to tiredness.

'I'm fine, Uncle Matt. Don't worry about me. Let's get you sorted out.' Smiling, she deliberately changed the subject. 'Would you like me to ask Dr Stratton to come in?'

Matt Wainwright suppressed a tiny sigh of exasperation. 'Why not? No point in keeping him in suspense.'

Taking a deep, controlling breath, Holly walked into the waiting-room. 'Dr Stratton?' She was momentarily disconcerted to find the seat vacant. 'Dr Stratton?' Advancing further into the room, she found Sam Stratton standing with his hands in his pockets, staring out of the window. She started as the tall figure turned, feeling her colour deepen as she took in the strong nose and firmly sculpted mouth.

One dark eyebrow rose. 'Dr Palmer?'

She was again conscious of every line of the taut, muscular body in the expensively tailored suit. Sam Stratton was a fraction over six feet tall, aged about thirty-five, and aggressively masculine.

She swallowed hard. 'I'm sorry, you made me jump. I didn't see you standing there.'

'It's snowing again.'

'It's probably setting in for the winter. You get used to it—learn to adapt.' She tried not to stare at the way his dark hair brushed against his collar.

'I like the winter, especially Yorkshire winters. Snow adds a certain magical quality, don't you think? I like the ruggedness of the countryside.'

He would, she thought. Her gaze swept past him to the large flakes falling with an ominous steadiness outside the window. She reached for the light-switch, snapping it on. 'I'm afraid you'll have to forgive me,' she responded bluntly, 'if I don't share your romantic views. It adds a lot of extra hard work, especially when we have to get to some of the more outlying farms. Some of the smaller roads can be blocked for weeks.'

'I appreciate that.' Blue eyes regarded her with an unreadable expression. Only the tremor at the corner of his mouth suggested that he was amused. 'I suppose children never look at the practicalities, do they?'

Holly frowned, for the first time aware that his voice held just the faintest trace of the local accent. 'I seem to recall, during the interview, that you said you had local connections?'

'My grandparents. I spent a lot of time with them as a child, so I know the area quite well.'

'Yes, well——' her teeth grated on a smile '—that can certainly be an advantage.' She held open the door. 'If you'd care to join us in the office.'

Uncle Matt was on his feet as they returned. Smiling, he proferred his hand. 'Dr Stratton, I'm sorry we had to keep you waiting. I don't know whether Holly has told you, but we've decided that if you still want it, the jobs is yours.'

'In that case, I'm delighted to accept.'

The two men shook hands. 'Welcome to Radleigh.' There was no mistaking Uncle Matt's satisfaction as he said it. Holly proffered her own hand, conscious of the deep-set blue eyes appraising her with mocking amusement.

'It's good to be here, and to be made to feel so welcome.'

Was there just the slightest emphasis on the last words, as if he had read her mind? The thought was oddly disturbing. Holly released her hand sharply to make an exaggerated play of shuffling a pile of case-notes and returning medical journals to the shelf.

'Well, I have to admit, now that it's all settled, I feel an enormous sense of relief.' Matt poured more coffee, handing the cups around. 'Holly doesn't complain——' he smiled in her direction '—but I know things haven't been easy for her these past few months.'

'I gather you had a heart attack? I take it you've made a full recovery?'

'It was all a bit of a damn nuisance, that's all. I'm fine. Strong as an ox. I've never taken it easy in my life and I certainly don't intend to start now. What do doctors know, anyway?'

Holly joined in with the laughter, feeling her throat tighten as, for a few seconds, she became aware of a pair of shrewd blue eyes meeting hers.

'So, when can you start, then?' Her uncle was smiling.

'More or less immediately. I've completed my present contract and decided I'd take a spot of long-overdue leave, but I'd like to get started. Just name the day.'

Drinking her coffee, Holly stood at the window, taking a long look at Dr Sam Stratton. As he half sat, half stood against the desk, an indulgent smile showing his even, white teeth, she decided that he really was quite attractive, in a rugged sort of way. Not that he was her type, of course, but she could see why most women would fall for the dark good looks, with his clear-cut features and dark hair. Until now she hadn't noticed the tiny lines of tiredness edging his mouth, but they were there, adding a kind of ruthlessness which momentarily left her feeling vaguely shaky.

'What do you think, Holly?'

Colour flooded her cheeks as, with a start, she jerked back to the realisation that she was being addressed. 'I—I'm sorry?'

'Sam was offering to start a week from now. I think that should be fine, don't you?'

'Oh, yes, fine.'

'I just need a little time to get my things together and tie up a few loose ends.'

'What will you do about accommodation?' Matt was asking.

'No problem. I'll find something temporary, put up at the local pub maybe, until I find something with a short lease.'

'Mmm. . . Not exactly ideal, though, is it?' Matt frowned. 'Especially when you take night calls. Of course, there's always the cottage. It may not suit, but you might care to consider it.'

'Cottage?'

'Yes,' Matt enthused. 'Holly has two adjoining properties. She allows us to use the empty cottage for visiting locums, covering holiday periods and so on. It's still on offer, isn't it, my dear?'

She felt her heart sink. 'Well, yes, though it's very small. . .'

'It sounds ideal.'

Damn the man. Couldn't he take a hint? The colour rose in her cheeks. 'It's been empty for ages. It's probably damp.'

'I'm sure it will be fine.' His voice was pleasantly silky. 'I'll take it.'

'But. . .you haven't seen it yet.'

'I take it it has the usual facilities? A roof would be nice.'

'It's perfectly sound, structurally.' She chose to ignore his sarcasm. 'But it's been standing empty for months. It *is* probably damp, and it's certainly in need of repair.'

Blue eyes glinted. 'I've been known to do the odd

spot of DIY. Let's call it part of the tenancy agreement, shall we? How soon can I take a look?'

'Well, I. . .'

'No time like the present.' Matt consulted his watch as he rose to his feet. 'I can cover here, my dear, take the odd phone call. We're relatively quiet. You two go ahead.'

With an effort Holly forced a smile to her lips as she gathered up her jacket, shrugged herself into it, draped a scarf round her neck and made for the door. 'In that case, I'll see you at my car in about ten minutes, Dr Stratton.' She shot a look at Uncle Matt and saw a tiny smile tugging at his mouth as if he was actually enjoying himself, though why, she couldn't imagine. 'I'll be back in plenty of time for afternoon surgery.'

'I thought it might be easier if we take my car. It will give me a chance to find my way around. You don't mind, do you?'

She jumped as a hand came beneath her elbow. In a small, nervous gesture she ran a hand through her hair. 'No, of course not.'

It wasn't a small car, but she was still aware of him, too close, could smell the distinctive aftershave he was wearing as she climbed reluctantly into the passenger seat. She averted her eyes, concentrating on the fields, the thin covering of snow that was already settling.

'I'm sorry you're not happy about me being here, joining the practice.'

Her head jerked up. 'I didn't say that.'

'You didn't have to.' Humour tinged his voice. 'You have a remarkably expressive face, Dr Palmer. The question is, why?'

She cleared her throat. 'Why?'

'I take it there is a reason? Something I've inadvertently done—or said.'

'Not at all. I told you, it was just that. . .'

'Your vote would have gone to Dr Forbes and you were overruled.'

Her chin lifted. 'I think you should understand, Dr Stratton, Uncle Matt and I support each other one hundred per cent.'

He raised a hand in mock protest. 'I'm sure you do. I'm not looking for a fight. I'd just like to feel I was welcome here.'

Holly looked at him sharply. 'Why exactly are you here? I mean, the real reason. We're hardly what you're used to.' She directed him into a narrow lane. 'The cottages are ahead about half a mile. Why would you, why would anyone, want to leave a nice, bright, modern hospital for—for this?' She gestured briefly in the direction of the open fields. 'This is another world.'

'Maybe that's why.'

It was almost a relief when they drew up at the roadside. The cottages, built of local stone, were set back slightly, beyond a small gate leading to a garden devoid of colour now, but where birds gathered to feed at a well-stocked table.

He drew the car to a halt, cut the engine, but made no attempt to get out.

'Things are changing. It's a tough world out there.' He turned to look at her and she had to stifle a sudden and totally illogical feeling that his presence somehow made the car seem smaller. 'Medical care is big business these days, Dr Palmer, or hadn't you noticed? When finance and power-politics take over it's all too easy to forget what real medicine is all about. Bright, shiny hospitals are one thing, but where does the patient fit into the scale of priorities? That was the question I was more and more having to ask myself, and I didn't particularly like the answers I was getting.'

Holly shifted uneasily. 'I suppose I can understand that.'

He raised one dark eyebrow and turned to stare through the windscreen. 'I doubt if you realise it fully yet, but you will. There's still a lot of space out there, but it's gradually being swallowed up. It happens so slowly that you may not even be aware of it and then, before you know it, everything is changed. Values change. Priorities change. Money is what becomes important and that's a rationale I find hard to live with.'

The note of bitterness in his voice shook her, yet she knew what he meant. Radleigh was a beautiful small market town, but for how much longer?

'I hope you don't imagine a rural practice will be a sinecure, Dr Stratton? Being isolated brings its own problems.' She climbed out, shivering and tugging the collar of her jacket together as he uncoiled himself from the car to stand beside her.

'The name is Sam,' he said evenly, 'and I'm not looking for an easy life, just something different from the rat-race. It has to exist somewhere. This is as close as I've come.'

Digging his hands into his pockets, he followed as she fumbled with the lock. Her hands were cold and she dropped the keys. 'Damn!'

'Here, let me.' He took them from her as she straightened up. Holly averted her eyes from his hands. They were strong and tanned. Dark hair shadowed his wrists as he pushed the door open and stood aside, allowing her to enter.

She did so, standing in silence as his gaze swept the large open fireplace, the comfortable, if slightly old-fashioned furnishings. She said anxiously, 'It's cold in here. I did warn you it's probably damp. I try to keep it heated, but. . .'

'Don't worry about it. It's nothing a good roaring fire won't put right.' He moved to the window, pulled back the curtains and peered out before crossing to one of the doors. 'I take it this is the kitchen?'

'It's fairly small, I'm afraid, and mind your h——' She winced as his head made sharp contact with a low beam. 'Sorry, I should have warned you.'

He grimaced wryly. 'I'll get used to it. I guess folk were a bit shorter when these places were built.'

It obviously hadn't occurred to him that, at something over six feet, he was exceptionally tall. Holly looked at him, then quickly averted her eyes, concentrating instead on the compact but surprisingly adequate kitchen. 'I think you'll find everything you need. If not, just ask.'

'It'll be fine. I don't tend to spend a lot of time in the kitchen.' He gave a slight and surprisingly attractive smile. 'I'm not the world's best cook. As long as there's a can-opener.'

A damning reflection on his wife, Holly thought. Assuming, of course, that there was a wife.

'How about the bedrooms?'

Her heels clicked across the floor. She straightened cushions as she went, trying to ignore the slightly threadbare rug and curtains which had faded with the sun. She had been meaning to do something about them, but somehow she had never quite summoned up the enthusiasm. 'There are two.' She indicated a door leading to the stairs. 'One small, the other not so small. It will just about take a double bed. I—I suppose you'd like to see. . .'

He smiled. 'I'll take your word for it.' He wandered around the room, touching surfaces, looking at the few impersonal ornaments she had scattered around. As she saw it suddenly through a stranger's eyes every shortcoming seemed to acquire a new dimension. What must he think of it?

Holly bit her lip. 'I'm sorry there isn't a great deal in the way of furniture. I can always——'

'It's fine. I like it the way it is.' He ran a hand appreciatively over the small antique writing-bureau. 'Someone obviously has a good eye.'

She flushed. 'I like to browse at sales. I'm no expert. I tend to go by instinct.'

Blue eyes met hers. 'I find that's the best way with most things, don't you?'

Right now her instincts were giving her a hard time. She moistened her dry lips. 'Yes, well, is there anything else I can show you? Any questions you'd like to ask? If not. . .'

'Why two?' He turned slowly and she could feel the blue eyes studying her.

'I beg your pardon?'

'Why two cottages?'

She drew her breath and turned away, making a play of rearranging the curtains. 'It seemed like a good idea at the time. The owner of this particular cottage died. She was elderly and there were no relatives. The one next door had been empty for some time. We bought the two together, at a pretty competitive price, intending to work on the renovations and eventually make the two cottages into one larger property. It just. . . We. . . didn't get around to it.'

'We?'

Holly swallowed hard. 'Martin, my husband, and I.'

Sam smiled. 'So, what happened? The funds run out, or the enthusiasm?'

Her fingers tightened spasmodically. 'Martin was killed, just over two years ago.'

Some emotion flared briefly in the depths of his blue eyes. 'I'm sorry. I didn't know.'

'There's no reason why you should.'

His mouth tightened. 'What happened? Or would you rather not talk about it?'

'It was a motorcycle accident.' She forced herself to look at him directly. 'Martin was something of a fanatic about them. He bought the bike just after we were married. I wasn't too happy about it, but I suppose it made sense. He was working at the hospital at the time. I'd just joined the practice here with Uncle Matt. Martin insisted I use the car and he used his bike for getting to and from work, not that he needed an excuse.' Her mouth twisted. 'He'd been saving up for it when we were both medical students.'

'He was a doctor?'

Holly nodded. 'He was a few years ahead of me in training. We'd practically grown up together—well, lived in the same village, went to the same schools.' She smiled slightly. 'It was actually Martin's idea that I should go the whole hog and become a doctor. I'd planned on nursing.'

'I take it you have no regrets?'

She moved over to the fireplace, struck a match and bent to light the fire which had been laid already. For a few seconds she held her hands out to the flames. 'This should help to air the place. Regrets?' She lifted her head to look at him. 'No, not about that, anyway. I enjoy general practice. It wasn't Martin's cup of tea. He wanted to specialise, in orthopaedics. He'd just been offered a post as registrar——' She broke off.

'You don't have to go on. I shouldn't have asked.'

Sighing, she straightened up. 'It's all right. I don't mind talking about it.'

'You couldn't have been married long?'

'Just over two years.'

'You've never thought of selling?' Sam bent to place a log in the flames.

'No, not yet. Maybe some time.'

His mouth twisted. 'Well, I'm glad. When can I move in?'

She stared at him, fighting a sudden and totally illogical feeling of panic. 'Surely you'll want to think about it? Discuss it with someone—your wife?'

He straightened up and she saw the cool amusement in his eyes. 'There's nothing to think about and I'm not married, so there's no one to consult.'

She felt the colour rising in her cheeks. 'I'm sorry. I didn't mean to pry.'

'No problem,' he said evenly. 'Since we're going to be working together we may as well get the niceties out of the way. As a matter of fact, there's another reason why I wanted to move. I'd been living with a girl for about three years, until she met someone else.'

'I'm sorry.'

'Don't be. The writing had been on the wall for some time. We both knew it. We just hadn't put it into words, that's all.' He shrugged. 'I suppose we both wanted different things. Basically we hadn't been seeing too much of each other lately, what with my hours at the hospital and Lisa's commitments at the gallery.'

'Gallery? She wasn't in the medical profession, then?'

'Lord, no.' He laughed, a deep-throated and surprisingly pleasant sound. 'Lisa works for the art department of one of the big auction houses. She's good at her job. Too good to want to give it up. I wanted out of the rat-race, so. . .things just came to a head.' Holly was disconcerted to discover that he had somehow moved closer. 'And here we are, as they say.'

'I hope you're not going to have regrets, Dr Stratton.' Holly looked up sharply. 'For Uncle Matt's sake, this practice needs someone who's prepared to give one hundred per cent commitment. If you have any doubts, any second thoughts. . .?' She paused for breath and his laser-blue eyes narrowed, sending tiny ripples of shock running through her. Then, before she knew what was happening, he had bent his head and his lips lightly brushed against her own.

'Shall we just say that's to seal the contract? I hate to disappoint you, Dr Palmer, but I'm here to stay, for the next few months at least. The sooner you get used to the idea, the better.' He released her immediately and looked at his watch. 'I'd better get back. There are things I need to sort out if I'm going to move in next week. I'll wait in the car while you lock up.'

Without waiting to see the effect his words had had, he turned on his heel and walked away, but not before she had seen the gleam of amusement in his eyes.

Her mouth tightened. Well, really! There was such a thing as taking neighbourliness too far. Gathering up her bag, she checked that the fire was safe and snapped off the light. What on earth had she let herself in for? It was galling to discover that her hands were actually shaking as she found the key and inserted it into the lock. This was ridiculous! She only had to work with the man; she didn't have to like him.

So what was it about Sam Stratton that was making her so irrationally edgy? Breathing hard, she marched angrily towards the car. Climbing into the car, she snapped the seatbelt firmly into place and turned to stare out of the window, telling herself decisively that she wouldn't think about it.

She had spent the two years since Martin's death trying to pick up the pieces, and was just beginning to get her life into some sort of order. She didn't need Sam Stratton's particular brand of arrogance; she didn't need the kind of disruption she just knew he was going to cause. But it wasn't that simple. Working with the man was easy—she could still maintain a distance—but having him as a neighbour? Now that was quite a different kettle of fish!

CHAPTER TWO

WITHIN the space of a week, winter had set in with a vengeance. Stifling a jaw-cracking yawn, Holly stood at the kitchen sink watching the birds forage hungrily for food as she drained her mug of coffee and tried to force her brain into gear.

A large black cat wandered into the kitchen to rub against her legs, purring loudly. 'I suppose you want to go out?' Holding open the door, she shivered as a blast of cold air blew in. Thomas peered out disdainfully and backed away. 'Mmm. . . I can't say I blame you. I wouldn't mind curling up on a chair in front of the fire myself, but some of us have to go to work.'

She checked her appearance briefly in the mirror, approving the full, calf-length skirt, neatly belted at the waist over a tan-coloured polo-necked sweater. Her briefcase was on the table where she had left it when she had finally returned from a call at about two-thirty in the morning, too tired even to make herself a cup of tea before falling back into a cold bed.

'Behave yourself.' She stroked the cat's sleek black fur. 'The new neighbour moves in today and he may not take kindly to uninvited visitors, so you'd better start minding your manners.'

Thomas flicked his tail in the air before haughtily stalking away. 'I know how you feel,' Holly admonished, 'but we've got to make the best of it. We need him, for Uncle Matt's sake.'

Her jacket was beside her briefcase. Barely flicking a comb through her hair, she went out to the car, gasping as a wave of freezing air hit her lungs. Fumbling with her keys, she felt her heart miss a beat as she saw the sports-car parked at the side of the cottage. He was here, then. She wondered when he had arrived, surprised she hadn't heard it.

As she stood hesitating a tall figure appeared from the doorway of the neighbouring cottage, his arms full of crushed cardboard boxes. Dressed in jeans and an Arran-type sweater, there was an aura of powerful masculinity about Sam Stratton that took her breath away.

'Good morning.'

'Good morning.' She felt oddly flustered. 'I wasn't expecting you until later.'

'There didn't seem any reason to hang around once I'd got my stuff together.' He tossed the boxes into the car, the flexing of his muscles disturbingly evident as he did so. 'Besides, the sooner I get sorted out, the sooner I can start pulling my weight at the practice.'

'There's no great panic.'

'I'm sure there's not, but I know from experience this is one of the busiest times of the year.'

Her lips tightened. 'I manage.'

'I'm sure you do. I wasn't implying any criticism,' he said evenly. 'What time did you get back from your call this morning?'

'About two-th——' She broke off, frowning. 'How did you. . .?'

'Easy.' He slammed the car door and nodded towards her own vehicle. 'That's just about when it started snowing again. The ground under your car is almost clear.'

'Oh, very clever. A detective, no less.'

Blue eyes regarded her with amusement. 'I'll see you later.' He held the door of her car open and she struggled in. In the process her body brushed against his, sending a crazy shock-wave running through her.

Startled, she grasped her briefcase from his outstretched hand, tossed it on to the back seat, slammed the door and drove away, leaving him standing in the snow.

The road was rutted with ice and it needed all her powers of concentration to keep the car steady. It was slow going, with the result that by the time she arrived at the surgery the waiting-room was full.

Letting herself in by the back door, she made her way through reception, collecting the morning's mail and pausing to peer at the waiting-list. She groaned.

'That's all I need.'

'Bad night?'

'What night?'

'Uh-oh.' Julie Clegg, the practice receptionist, grinned as she reached for the phone, adding yet another name to the list. 'Right, Mrs Benson, if you'd like to bring young Lucy along to the surgery. Yes, I'm afraid we are pretty busy, so you may have a bit of a wait, but, yes, Doctor will definitely take a look at her this morning. Lovely, we'll see you later, then.' Replacing the receiver, she looked at Holly. 'Like that, is it?'

'You could say. I got a call to Wally Briggs's place. He doesn't look too good. I got him admitted to hospital with chest pains, query heart attack. Which reminds me, I'll give them a ring later and check on his progress.'

'I bet Maggie's pretty upset.'

'Panic-stricken. No, that's not quite true. She's bearing up marvellously, but you can see it's knocked her for six. Old Wally's hardly had a day's illness in his life. Summer or winter, he's out on the farm with his dogs, watching those sheep of his. He seemed as fit as a fiddle until now. Oh, lord, look at the time.' Holly reached for the batch of cards. 'I'd better make a start if I'm going to finish this side of lunchtime.'

Julie smiled sympathetically. 'I bet you can hardly wait for the new chap to arrive? This week, isn't it? It's going to make life so much easier all round, having someone else to share the workload. I only met Dr Stratton briefly——' her brown eyes twinkled '—but he seems very nice, and so good-looking too.'

Holly said briskly, 'Yes, well, I wouldn't know about that. At least now Uncle Matt should be able to take things easy with a clear conscience, or at least, that's the theory.' She frowned. 'I don't suppose you could drum up a cup of strong, black coffee, could you?'

'Leave it to me. Two sugars?'

'Better make it three.' Turning away, she almost collided with the slim, navy-clad figure emerging from the small treatment-room.

'Oh, hi, Holly, I'm glad I caught you. Can you spare a minute?'

'Yes, sure, come in.'

Kate Pearson, the practice nurse, followed Holly into the consulting-room. 'It's about the well woman clinic.'

'Is there a problem?' Holly dumped her briefcase on the desk and hung up her jacket.

'Well, not a problem really, it's just that several of our ladies have mentioned that mornings are not a good time for them. Afternoons would be better, and I know what they mean. Oh, the clinic is a great idea. . .'

'It's certainly proved to be pretty popular since we started it twelve months ago,' Holly smiled. 'I hadn't really anticipated quite how popular.'

'That's the problem.' Kate gave a rueful smile. 'Mornings are our busiest time. I like to be able to spend a bit of time with each patient. It's not just a matter of doing the smear tests. Some of the older ones want to talk about hormone replacement treatment, or menopausal problems, and the truth is, I just don't always have as much time as I'd like.'

'Mmm, I know what you mean. So, what do you suggest?'

'Well, moving the clinic to the afternoon would be better.'

'That's fine with me. I have the ante-natal clinic on Fridays. I suppose we could fit both in. In fact, that might work out quite well, bearing in mind, of course, that Dr Stratton will be alternating clinics with me. But if he's in agreement. . .'

'Ah.' Kate grinned. 'Well, actually, I've already mentioned it to him.'

'You have? When?'

'Well, we met when he came for his interview, of course, and I showed him round. We had a bit of a chat, and then he phoned in early this morning. He's dishy, by the way, and he says he's all for making the change. In fact, he says he has a few ideas of his own he'd like to discuss, after he's spoken to you, of course.'

'Oh, has he, indeed?' Holly found herself battling against a feeling of resentment. 'Well, we'll see about that.' Clearly Dr Sam Stratton was going to need some watching. At this rate, given half a chance, he'd be taking over the practice!

All in all, the morning passed remarkably quickly. There was the inevitable spate of coughs and sore throats, most of which could be treated simply with Disprin and the old-fashioned but still useful remedy of honey and lemon, though a few required antibiotics. There was an ingrown toenail, a slipped disc, and a little light relief as Holly was able to confirm a pregnancy.

'Are you quite sure?' Cathy Stevenson was forty-two years old, married for a second time, and already had two strapping sons of eighteen and sixteen.

Holly laughed as she washed her hands and returned

to sit at the desk. 'Absolutely. I'd say you're about twelve weeks.'

'Well, I'm blowed. And to think I'd been putting it down to a spot of heartburn.'

'It's one of the classic symptoms.' Holly glanced at the notes in front of her. 'I take it you're pleased? There's going to be quite a gap between this one and the others, isn't there?'

'I'll let you know when I've had a chance to take it in.' Cathy Stevenson eyed her with amusement. 'Aye, of course I am really. It's just a bit of a shock, that's all. I mean, with the lads grown up and all.'

'I see you remarried—what—nearly a year ago?'

'That's right.'

'I take it your husband will be pleased about the baby?'

'Ken? He'll just have to get used to the idea, won't he?' She chuckled. 'He'll be fine. Mind, I'll have to sit him down and maybe give him a good stiff drink before I tell him.'

Holly smiled. 'I take it the baby wasn't exactly planned.'

The woman blushed slightly. 'You could say it's a bit of an accident. At my age I wasn't planning on having any more. We went to my niece's wedding. I suppose we celebrated too much and got a bit careless.' Her expression became one of concern. 'It'll be all right, won't it? I mean, there's bound to be them who'll say I'm past it and shouldn't be thinking about babies at my time of life.'

'What other people say isn't really important.' Holly smiled. 'Obviously there are certain risks when an older woman becomes pregnant. The instances of Down's syndrome are increased, but these days there are tests we can do.'

'It won't make any difference. We'd still want it, I mean.'

'Yes——' Holly smiled '—I can see that. But you need to be aware of the risks and it's my duty, as your doctor, to point them out to you. Look——' she completed her notes '—let's start by getting you booked in for your monthly antenatal clinics. You'll also need an appointment to see the consultant at the hospital. He'll check the progress of your pregnancy, you'll have a routine scan, usually at eighteen weeks, and he'll arrange for an amniocentesis—that's the test for Down's syndrome. By the way, you don't smoke, do you?'

'No. Well, at least not for the past ten years.'

'Good, because evidence seems to support the theory that women who smoke have smaller babies and there's also a heightened risk of cot death. In any case, the baby will do much better after it's born if it isn't inhaling lungfuls of smoke. Still, I can see I'm preaching to the converted. So, I'll see you in a month's time, or before, if you have any worries at all.'

Watching her leave, Holly experienced a tiny stab of emotion she had never experienced before, almost a feeling of. . . Surely it couldn't be jealousy, she told herself briskly as her hand reached for the bell. She and Martin had wanted children, of course, but it had seemed practical to wait. She had been newly qualified and still had her year as a houseman to do when they had decided to get married. Children were part of the future; the future that had never arrived—not for Martin, anyway. Her hand came sharply down on the bell again.

The door opened and one of the local mums ushered in her two youngsters.

'Molly.' Holly took a deep breath, instinctively shifted everything even remotely movable out of reach and smilingly invited the harassed-looking young woman to sit. 'Come in and tell me what I can do for you.'

'Well, I seem to be feeling so tired all the time, and I've got this headache.'

I can believe it, Holly thought as she viewed the pale face of the woman in front of her, and noted the lethargic movements as she tried to restrain a boisterous three-year-old.

Holly had known the Danielses for some time. They had moved into the nearby village about four years ago when Steve Daniels had gone to work on one of the local farms as a cowman.

Though always hard-working, he had lost his job in the town—a job he had never liked—and after six months unemployment had leapt at the chance of a job where he could work outdoors rather than cooped up in a factory. The whole family had settled in happily. Things had seemed to be going so well that it came as something of a shock to Holly to see her patient looking uncharacteristically under the weather.

'How long have you been feeling like this, Molly?'

'Oh. . .a while. Peter, don't do that.' She tugged ineffectively at the four-year-old. 'I'm sorry. He's not usually naughty, just a bit lively.'

Holly smiled. 'Yes, I can see that. Don't worry about it. You say you have a headache. When is it worse?'

'Well, it's there all the time, really.'

'And when did you first begin to notice it?'

The woman sighed. Her fingers picked restlessly at the coat of the child who was held, squirming, on her knee. 'Look, it's nowt, really. I take a few aspirins. . .'

Holly let that pass while making a note. 'And how are you sleeping?'

'Not too well. Oh, I get off to sleep all right, the

minute my head touches the pillow—well, these two keep me on the go all day.'

'I'm sure they do.'

'It's waking up in the early hours, you know? I'm lying there wide awake, thinking. I know it's daft. I'm tired—worn out. Sometimes I creep downstairs and make a cup of tea so as not to disturb Steve.'

Holly pushed her chair back and looked at the pale, drawn features. 'Are you worrying about anything in particular?'

The woman looked away, stroking her son's hair. She gave a slight laugh. 'You know how it is when you've got children. They never give you a minute's peace, always up to something.'

'I can appreciate that.' Holly smiled gently. 'I know it can't be easy.' She twirled the pen she was holding. 'How is Steve? I haven't seen him around for some time.'

'He's. . .fine.'

'Still enjoying his work?'

Molly Daniel's face crumpled. Fumbling for a hanky, she blew her nose hard. 'Oh, aye, he's enjoying it all right, for as long as it lasts.'

Holly saw the brightness of tears in the woman's eyes. She said quietly, 'Can you tell me about it?'

'There's not much to tell.' The children had stopped creating havoc and were anxiously watching their mother. 'It seems as if we just find our feet and something else comes along to knock us back again.'

'Molly, are you saying his job is at risk?'

'Aye,' came the weary response. 'Leastways, that's how it looks, and it's a damn shame.' She wiped her eyes and sniffed hard. 'It's not Jack Burrows's fault. He's getting on and he's not been right since he took that fall on the tractor six months back.'

Holly frowned. 'Yes, I remember. It was pretty nasty. It was your Steve who found him, wasn't it?'

'That's right. Jack was out in the field. Steve was busy with the cows. Come teatime he realised Jack wasn't back, so he went to look for him and found him lying pinned under the tractor where it had turned over.'

'He's lucky Steve didn't waste any time getting the emergency services out. But I thought Jack had made a full recovery?'

'Oh, yes, he has—well, more or less. He's a bit nervy, you know, and like I say, he's getting on. I reckon he still misses Rose.'

'His wife.'

Molly Daniels nodded. 'I don't think he's looking after himself properly. I call in to see him from time to time and Steve keeps an eye out, quietly like, but. . .' She shook her head. 'He's talking about selling up the farm and moving to live with his daughter down south somewhere.'

Holly bit at her lower lip. 'I hate to say it, but I'd breathe a sigh of relief if he did decide to take things more easily. That doesn't help you and Steve, though, does it? Oh, Molly, I'm really sorry. I can see why you're so worried. Isn't there a chance that the new owner might keep Steve on? He's a good worker.'

'Oh, we know that, and Jack knows how worried we are, but it's not going to be easy to find a buyer. In the meantime, things are getting more and more run down. And then there's the cottage. It's tied, so it goes with the job.'

She slid the child to his feet, stood up and started buttoning her coat. 'Look, I'm sorry. I shouldn't have bothered you with this. . .'

'Nonsense. That's what I'm here for. Besides, I know you and Steve well enough to know you're not time-wasters.' She sat forward. 'I know this is a time of stress for you both, but I really am loath to start you on a course of antidepressants. They would certainly make you feel better, for a while, but they won't make the problems go away. What I can do is to let you have some mild sleeping-tablets. If you can get a good night's sleep, chances are you'll feel more able to cope with things during the day, including this pair.'

Ruffling the two blond heads, Holly handed the woman a prescription and rose to her feet. 'I hope things work out, but if you need to talk again, I'm here, any time.'

Having seen the family out, Holly tidied her desk and gathered up her jacket.

'All finished?' Julie smiled.

'For now, anyway.' Passing through Reception, Holly handed over the case-notes and looked at her watch.

'By the way, I thought you should know, your uncle is in.'

'Oh, no!'

''Fraid so. I was just making him some coffee.'

'Great idea. I'll take it in and give him a talking-to. He knows he's not supposed to be here.'

Julie grinned as the phone rang. 'Best of luck. Hello, Mrs Rogers. Yes, of course. . .'

Holly left her to it, carrying the steaming mug of coffee as she made her way along the corridor. Tapping on the door, she popped her head round.

'Hi, what are you doing here?'

Matthew Wainwright looked up, smiling. 'No more than usual. I thought I could do a bit of paperwork. Come in.'

'You know you're not supposed to be here,' she chastised gently. 'Here, I come bearing gifts.' She set the mug of coffee on the desk. 'The paperwork can wait, you know.'

'I just needed something to do, that's all.' He reached into his pocket and slipped an indigestion tablet into his mouth.

Holly looked at him keenly. 'How are you? You're not. . .'

'I'm fine, fine.' He waved her query away. 'Touch of indigestion, that's all. Haddock for breakfast. I should have known better. How about you? Busy morning?'

She went along with what she knew was a deliberate change of subject. 'You could say, and it's not over yet. I've got a few calls to make on the way home. Still, at least there's no surgery this afternoon, so, barring any emergencies——' she smiled wryly '—I intend having a long soak in a hot bath and putting my feet up this evening.'

Matt followed her to the door. 'At least things should ease up a little now, with Sam starting tomorrow. Oh, and by the way, I thought it might be a good idea to bring the weekly practice meeting forward. It might give him a chance to see what goes on, and put in a few ideas of his own, maybe—unless Wednesday is a problem for you?'

'No.' She smiled slightly. 'Wednesday's fine. Look, I must dash. I want to call in at Raglet Farm after I've done my visits. Dorrie Simpson phoned the surgery. . .'

Matt frowned. 'Harry Boycott's neighbour?'

'Mmm, that's right. You know she keeps an eye on the old man? Well, she's not too happy about him. Nothing she can put her finger on, except that she thinks he's not eating properly and he looked a bit flushed last night. I thought I'd pop in and check him over, just to be on the safe side. He is eighty-two, after all.'

'I know. A cantankerous old cuss, is old Harry.' Matt smiled. 'He won't thank you for "interferin'" as he puts it.'

'No, I don't suppose he will.' Holly grinned. 'But I'd

better take a look, all the same. Dorrie's a sensible woman. She's looked out for him for the past ten years, and if she says she's worried I know she has cause. Anyway——' she swung her weight away from the desk '—I'm off. I'll see you tomorrow, and take it easy.'

Driving was almost a pleasure as the car wended its way out of the town and across the dales. A wintry sun sparkled on the virgin snow blanketing the fields and roadside. The temperature had scarcely risen above freezing all morning and now, past noon, was already beginning to drop again.

Parking her car in the farmyard, Holly tugged on her boots and made her way across to the stone-built house. The door opened as she reached it.

'Doctor.' Dorrie Simpson's weathered features beamed a welcome. 'I saw you drive up. Come in out of the cold. I've just made a pot of tea, and me and Ted were about to have a spot of lunch. It's home-made soup. Will you join us?'

'Dorrie, you're a life-saver. I'd love to.'

One of the first lessons Holly had quickly learned, when she had joined Matt in general practice, was that in this part of the country socialising wasn't a waste of time. It was often the best way of finding out about local problems. Even though she had lived here all her life, apart from the spell away when she had been doing her medical training, it had taken her a while to discover that, as a doctor, she had to win people's confidence and trust. The people were friendly without being intrusive, cared about their neighbours, looking out for the elderly, and were often the means of providing Holly with the first warning of impending trouble. Many a time she had had cause to be grateful.

Seated at the well-scrubbed kitchen table, with a fire crackling in the hearth and a steaming bowl of soup in front of her, she listened as the husband and wife voiced their fears about their neighbour.

'You said you saw Harry last night?'

'Aye, that's right. I always pop in last thing to see he's settled, like. He usually sits in front of the fire and dozes after his evening meal. Sometimes the light doesn't go out until after midnight.'

'Only last night when Dorrie went over, he was in bed.' Ted Simpson topped up Holly's cup with fresh tea.

'It's not like him, Doctor. He's not one for his bed.'

Holly frowned. 'No, it's not. I thought it best to come and have a little chat with you both first. . .'

'You won't get any sense out of Harry, that's for sure.'

'No, I know he can be stubborn. Can you tell me how he seemed?'

'Well, it's all a bit vague really.' Dorrie's face crumpled into lines of anxiety. 'I hope I'm not wasting your time.'

'I shall be quite happy if you are.' Holly offered smiling reassurance. 'Tell me what you can.'

'Well, as I say, he just didn't seem right. He said he'd not felt too well the day before, so he'd decided to stay in bed. From the look of him, I'd say something had been brewing for a while, but he's not one to let on.' Dorrie pushed her plate away. 'I took him a spot of dinner over as usual, but when I went back later to collect the dishes he hadn't eaten anything—said he was feeling a bit under the weather.'

'How did he look?'

Dorrie thought about it. 'A bit warm—mind, it were freezing in that old barn of a place. I made up the fire before I left and made sure he had something by the bed in case he wanted a drink. I thought maybe if he had a good night's sleep he'd be better, but this morning he's still in bed. He didn't want any breakfast, said he'd be up and about later, but there's been no sign, and usually we see him around.'

'Mmm. Well I think I'll pop over and take a look at him, just to be on the safe side. Would you come with me so that if anything needs doing I can explain to you and Harry together?'

Dorrie was already on her feet, shedding her apron. 'I'll get my coat.'

The old farmhouse seemed deserted as they crossed the neighbouring yard. Holly pushed open the door and called out, 'Harry, it's Dr Palmer. I've just called in to see if you're all right.'

There was no answer. As they advanced into the gloomy kitchen cold seemed to strike up from the old slate floor. The scrubbed table stood empty.

'He must still be in bed.' Having peered into the sitting-room, Holly made for the stairs, calling as she went, 'Harry, it's Dr Palmer.' The sound of coughing led her to a bedroom. Slowly pushing open the door, she peered through the deepening afternoon gloom to the bed, where a figure lay huddled beneath the blankets. They were lowered fractionally by a frail hand.

'I hear you're not feeling too well, Harry. I've got your neighbour, Dorrie Simpson, with me.' Holly moved closer to the bed. 'She's been a bit worried and called the surgery. What's the problem, Harry? Have you got a pain somewhere? Can I take a look?'

'It's me chest.' The thin, pale face was all that was visible above the covers. ''Tain't nothing to bother about. Bit of a cough, that's all.'

'Well, we'll see, shall we? Maybe we can make you a bit more comfortable.' Holly took her stethoscope from her case and sat on the edge of the bed. 'How long have you had the cough, Harry?'

''Bout a week.'

'Why didn't you let someone call me? You know I'd come out to see you any time.'

'Don't want to be no bother.'

Holly could hear the bubbling and wheezing even before she applied the stethoscope to his chest, and she felt her spirits drop. Thoroughly, but as quickly as possible, she made her examination. Having checked his blood-pressure and heart-rhythm, she sat back and looked at him.

'Well, you've got a chest infection, Harry, and it's not going to get any better without some help—you know that, don't you?'

'I ain't going to no hospital.'

Holly held back a sigh. 'I think you're going to have to, Harry, just for a few days anyway, so that they can give you regular medication and build you up a bit.' She looked gently into the watery eyes. 'You've not been looking after yourself and eating properly, have you?'

The thin hand flapped the question away. 'I'm not hungry.'

'No, but that's all part of the infection. We need to do something about it, Harry. You'll get better quicker if you go into hospital.'

'What about me animals?'

'Ted'll see to them.' Dorrie had been standing quietly in the background. 'He's been keeping an eye on them anyway, this past couple of days.'

Holly smiled gratefully. 'There you are, then, Harry. You've got nothing to worry about except getting better.' Rising to her feet, Holly folded her stethoscope back into her case. 'I'll make the arrangements.' She held the frail hand. 'I promise you, it will only be for a few days—a week at most. I'm just going to make a phone call, then I'll come back and tell you what's happening.'

'He's not so good, is he, Doctor?' Dorrie followed as Holly made her way downstairs.

In the kitchen, Holly reached for her mobile phone and keyed in the number of the local hospital. She shook her head. 'I'm afraid it might be pneumonia. If he were younger and in better shape I wouldn't be quite so worried, but——' She broke off as a voice responded at the other end of the phone, and within minutes had explained the situation and arranged for an ambulance to come out to the farm.

'He is going to be all right?'

'I hope so, Dorrie. I know he's not happy about going into hospital, but it really is for the best. I wouldn't like to accept the responsibility of keeping him here, even though I know you and Ted do more than your fair share of looking after him.'

'He's such a stubborn old cuss.'

Holly smiled. 'Well, that's one thing in his favour; he's a fighter.'

They crossed the yard together half an hour later, having watched the ambulance drive away.

'Will you have another cup of tea, Doctor?'

'I'd love to, but no thanks, Dorrie. I'd better make a move. I've still one more call to make, then I'm off home, hopefully to put my feet up.'

'Sounds like a good idea. How's your uncle?'

'Well, he says he's fine. I'm not so sure. But then, they say doctors make the worst patients. Anyway, I'm grateful to you and Ted. I couldn't have persuaded Harry to go to hospital if you hadn't been able to reassure him about his animals. I'll call you and let you know when he's due home.'

Holly waved as she turned the car, heading back towards the road. It was another hour, and dark, by the time she had finished the last call and finally headed for home.

The late afternoon air already struck with a deepening chill, heralding a frost. She felt tired as she turned her car into the lane heading towards the cottage, her spirits lifting briefly as a distant welcoming gleam of light came into view, until she remembered that it was coming from the cottage next door.

As she climbed out and locked the car door, the faint smell of cooking drifted tantalisingly to her nostrils. Her new neighbour had obviously wasted no time in making himself comfortable, thought Holly as she pushed open the kitchen door and fumbled for the switch.

A tiny, alien feeling of depression hit her as she shivered, realising the cottage was cold, which meant that the boiler must have gone out again. She had been meaning to get it serviced but had somehow never seemed to find the time to get around to arranging it. Like a lot of things these days.

She had been standing with her back pressed against the door, but now she drew herself up and moved purposefully towards the kitchen. Still wearing her jacket, she fumbled, shivering, to re-light the boiler before flicking the switch on the kettle.

'Thomas?' Chafing her hands, she went in search of the cat. He was probably curled up on her bed and she couldn't blame him. It was freezing in here.

The bedroom was empty. 'Thomas, I'm home,' she called. 'No answer was the firm reply,' she muttered as she went downstairs again. He must have gone out through the cat-flap. 'Crazy animal.' Opening the door, she peered into the freezing night air. 'Oh, well, more fool you, Thomas.

The ingredients for the casserole she had intended to make before leaving for work sat, untouched, on the work-surface. She had been too tired to think about food. Now her stomach rattled noisily in reproach, tormented by the smell wafting from next door. Damn the man! she thought, reaching into the fridge for a wedge of less-than-fresh cheese and switching on the toaster, fighting back a ridiculous urge to weep as she waited for it to heat.

An hour later, having showered and slipped a silk robe over her nightie, sitting on the ancient sofa with her feet tucked under her, a single lamp and the glow from a replenished fire casting a subdued light into the room, she stared into the flames, listening to the faint sound of classical music coming from next door. There was something vaguely reassuring about it.

Maybe she had become too used to her own company. In the first months following Martin's death she had dreaded coming home, walking into the emptiness, having no one except Thomas to talk to. After a while she had become reconciled—not happy, but more at ease with her own feelings; she had even managed not to feel guilty on days when she had actually found herself laughing aloud at something someone had said. More recently she had usually been too tired to think too deeply about anything.

Sighing, she rested her chin on her hand. If she was honest, maybe there could be some advantages to having Sam Stratton shoulder some of the burden at the practice.

She was taken unawares as a fleeting, but nonetheless disturbing image of Sam Stratton's attractive features flashed completely unbidden into her mind, and she wondered what it would be like to be married to such a man. The thought was crushed as swiftly as it rose. What was she doing, daydreaming about a man she hardly knew?

Her eyes must have closed because she started suddenly, jerking back to wakefulness and the realisation that someone was hammering at the door. Still half asleep, she went to open it, gasping as it let in a shaft of cold air.

She felt her heart miss a beat. Sam Stratton stood there. Faded jeans hugged his lean hips and thighs emphasising his maleness. Beneath his thin black sweat-shirt, his powerful shoulder muscles moved in taut definition.

He frowned. 'I was beginning to worry. I've been knocking for ages and couldn't get a reply.' His gaze narrowed slightly. 'Are you all right?'

'What? Oh, yes, I'm sorry.' She ran a hand through her hair. 'I must have fallen asleep. I didn't hear you.'

'Obviously not.' Flakes of snow had settled in his hair. His glance brushed over the robe she was wearing, and suddenly she was aware of how thin it was and how little she had on beneath it. 'I take it this belongs to you? I found him curled up on my bed.'

'Thomas!' She gave an exclamation of relief as she relieved him of a protesting Thomas, who objected strongly to being detached from the warmth of the black sweater. 'There you are. I've been looking every-where for you,' she said soothingly. 'You could have been frozen to death out there.'

'I know the feeling.' Blue eyes glinted. 'It must be about five below out here.'

She eyed him warily, then stepped back. 'I suppose you'd better come in,' she said ungraciously, leading the way to the kitchen where she set the cat down and gave him his dish of food. 'I apologise for Thomas. I'm afraid he's just a little bit spoilt. He used to belong to an elderly couple who doted on him. They died within a few months of each other. I'm afraid he must have found it something of a cultural shock, coming to me. He's not usually a terribly sociable animal.'

One dark eyebrow rose. 'You surprise me. He

seemed very friendly. In any case, I didn't say I minded. I just thought you might be worried.'

'Yes, well, I was rather. He's usually here waiting to meet me when I come in.'

'That's cats for you—totally disloyal.' He bent to stroke the animal and, as if to prove him right, Thomas began to purr loudly, arching his back against him. 'Is that Thomas as in Doubting?'

'As in Tank Engine,' Holly muttered.

'Mmm—I see what you mean.' Darting mockery laced the words. 'He is a shade on the large side.'

She felt her hackles rise, along with her defences. Standing here in a partial state of undress in the small kitchen wasn't doing anything for her peace of mind.

'I give him his daily requirement of vitamins and minerals,' she snapped. 'I can hardly be held responsible if he chooses to supplement it with the odd bird or mouse.' She clutched at the collar of her robe, drawing it together. 'I'll do my best to keep him under control in future.'

'Don't worry about it. I like cats.'

She stifled a yawn that made her eyes water. 'I'm sorry.'

A smile tugged at his mouth. 'Late nights play havoc. You never quite get used to it, do you? I remember there were some nights, especially when I was working in Accident and Emergency, when I seemed to get by on automatic pilot. How's the patient?'

She smiled slightly. 'I rang the hospital earlier. I think he's going to be OK.'

'The job does at least have its compensations.' His gaze narrowed slightly. 'I gather you've been doing all the night emergency calls? It can't have been easy.'

'Someone had to. I cope.' She frowned. 'The people round here are pretty considerate. They don't call unless they have to.'

'I wasn't criticising,' he said softly. He stood looking at her and she was suddenly uncomfortably aware of him as a man, and a very attractive man at that. 'You're worried about Matt, aren't you? He means a lot to you.'

'Of course he does.' She frowned, then shook her head. 'I suppose you could say he stood *in loco parentis* after my father died. My mother remarried a few years ago and went to live abroad. I suppose it was natural that Uncle Matt and I became close.' She swallowed hard, half turning away only to feel his hands on her shoulders, forcing her to look at him. She tried to pull away but he refused to let her. 'Of course I'm worried. He's not a young man. Oh, I know he says he's over it. . .'

'But you're not convinced.'

Holly bit at her lower lip and looked at him. 'He wants to get back to work. The doctors have told him he needs at least three months' convalescence.'

His gaze narrowed. 'I don't know him, but Matt seems to me like the kind of man who would resent being told to take things easy. He certainly wouldn't take happily to a life of inactivity.'

'You're right, but what can I do about it? I can't force him to take advice.'

His dark brows drew together. 'There isn't anything you can do, except perhaps be grateful that at least he realised he could lighten the load by bringing in some extra help. I'm only sorry you weren't happy about it.'

Colour flared in her cheeks. 'I didn't say that.'

Humour glinted in his eyes. 'I just wasn't sure whether it was me personally you took a dislike to or whether it was men in general.' His eyes narrowed to glittering blue slits. 'I got the distinct impression that Dr Forbes would, in your eyes, have been the lesser of several evils. Now, why is that, I wonder?'

Holly's gaze flew up to meet his and she found him regarding her with mocking amusement. Her cheeks flamed.

'Don't be ridiculous,' she snapped. 'I told you, I'd managed so far without any help. I could have gone on. . .'

'Matt obviously didn't think so,' he said evenly. 'I take it you've tried persuading him to take things more easily.'

She gave a slight laugh. 'Of course I've tried. Oh, he puts on a very convincing front, but I've seen him when he's really tired, when I've caught him off-guard.' She bit at her lip as she looked at him. 'He's been getting steadily worse in the past few weeks, more tired, more breathless. . .'

'That's why you agreed to a locum?'

'I had no choice. It was that or he would have insisted on getting back to work.'

His dark brows drew together. 'It's hardly surprising you're exhausted. How long did you think you could keep it up, Holly, covering surgeries as well as taking the emergency calls?'

'I'm stronger than I look,' she bridled defensively.

'No one's that strong, Holly.' His thumb brushed against her cheek, sending a strange riot of sensations running through her. 'I can understand how Matt feels. Given the same set of circumstances, if I were faced with the same decision, I know I'd want to carry on doing the job I love. I don't know how I'd stand the frustration of having to sit back and let someone else do it for me.'

Holly stared at him uneasily. 'So what do you suggest we do?'

Sam's gaze narrowed as he studied her appearance, seeing the faint shadows beneath her eyes. His gaze roamed from the soft tumble of her hair to the generous curve of her mouth, her features, devoid of any make-up, and the robe which clung just a shade too tightly. He said softly, 'I still say you don't look a day over eighteen.'

'I'm twenty-six, and you still haven't answered the question. What do we do?' She felt the colour surging into her cheeks as his gaze narrowed. 'About Uncle Matt, I mean.'

Her hands were against his chest, and she tried to push him away when his grasp tightened and he pulled her gently towards him. She was suddenly conscious of a crazy vortex of emotions that surged through her like a tidal wave as she looked up at him.

'I'd say we have no choice.' His mouth twisted into a smile. 'We've got to learn to get along together, Dr Palmer. Not just for your uncle's sake, but for the practice. I'm willing to give it a try. How about you? Can't we at least agree to be friends?'

Friends! The word seemed to stick in her throat. Somehow it wasn't a word she felt she could ever apply to her feelings about Sam Stratton.

Almost as if he read her thoughts, he said softly, 'Is it really so difficult, Holly?'

Her gaze flickered away from the amusement in his eyes. He smelled of expensive aftershave, and danger, even though she couldn't for the life of her have explained why.

'I'm sure we're both adult enough to behave professionally, Dr Stratton.'

She was almost certain she detected a hint of laughter in his voice.

'Absolutely.' His lips brushed against hers. Closing her eyes, she drew in a deep breath and somehow, without her even being aware of it, he had released her, and now he opened the door, letting in a fresh blast of cold air. 'I'll let you get to bed. Tomorrow is going to be a long day. Good night and sweet dreams. . . partner.'

It wasn't until she had switched out the lights and finally climbed into bed that Holly began to think serioiusly about what she had taken on. She didn't know anything about Sam Stratton, except that he seemed to provoke a great many conflicting emotions in her, emotions she had imagined were safely under control—until now.

CHAPTER THREE

'SORRY I'm late.' Breathlessly Holly put her briefcase on the floor in the small office. Her cheeks were flushed and she paused briefly to rest her frozen hands on the radiator. 'Oh, that's a relief. Have I missed anything?'

Julie shook her head, moving aside to make room. 'I only just got here myself. Wouldn't you just know it? Any other morning I can at least take off my coat before the phone starts ringing, but when it's the morning for our practice meeting, I can guarantee it will start the second I walk through the door.'

'Mmm—I know what you mean.' Holly felt her gaze drawn involuntarily to where Sam stood at the window, engaged in an animated conversation with Kate. He looked quite different in the dark suit instead of the faded jeans. She watched as he threw back his head, giving a deep-throated laugh, until, absorbed in her critical survey, she suddenly became aware that his own blue eyes were appraising her in return.

It was a disconcerting feeling. Illogically, it made her want to check that a wisp of hair hadn't escaped its restraining clip. Instead, blushing slightly, she was glad when Matt spoke.

'I think perhaps we'd better get started if we're going to finish this meeting before morning surgery. Help yourselves to coffee if you want it, everyone, and make yourselves comfortable.' He waved them all to seats.

Juggling her cup, briefcase and a stack of mail, Holly had half turned to ease her way into a seat when the bundle of letters began to slide from her grasp, cascading on to the floor.

49

'Damn!' Annoyed by her own carelessness, she bent to retrieve them, colliding heavily with another figure as it followed suit. She swayed, and instinctively Sam reached out, grasping her arms, steadying her as he straightened up.

'Here, you'd better let me.' In one easy movement he gathered up the letters, placing them in her hands. 'No harm done.' His eyes glinted and Holly felt the breath catch in her throat as a feeling of physical awareness swept through her.

'Thanks.'

He inclined his head in acknowledgement. 'Sleep well?'

A small pulse began to hammer in her throat. 'Like a log, thank you.' She withdrew her hands from his grasp, but not before she had seen his mouth curve in silent laughter.

'I'd thought of changing the practice meeting to another day,' Matt was saying, 'but then, it seems as good a way as any for Sam to get a picture of what we have to deal with, on a day to day basis, and any problems we might be likely to come up against. Apart from that, we're all busy people. It may sound daft but these weekly meetings are often the only chance we get to talk to each other, air any small worries before they turn into big grievances.'

'It sounds like a good system to me,' Sam said easily.

'So, has anyone got any specific worries?'

'Paperwork,' Betty, the practice manager pronounced, amid a communal groan. Her expression defied anyone to argue. 'I don't invent it,' she declared roundly. 'Presumably you've read your GP contract. If you don't do your paperwork, the practice doesn't get paid.' She eyed Matt meaningfully. 'That includes claims for minor surgery work.' At fifty, Betty had acquired a reputation for being something of a dragon.

It was unfair and unwarranted. She ran the practice like clockwork and was, at heart, as soft as butter. She simply didn't feel it paid to let on because, 'if you did, there's always folks who'll be happy to take advantage.'

'I'll see to it, I'll see to it,' Matthew Wainwright mumbled docilely.

Sam frowned. 'I gather you became a fund-holding practice about six months ago.'

'This was discussed with you at interview.' Holly stiffened defensively.

'I'm not complaining.' Sam raised an amused eyebrow. 'On the contrary, I'm all for it. In fact, that was one of the reasons I liked the look of this particular practice. I was simply wondering how you feel it's working out?'

'We're very happy with it, so far,' Matt put in. 'We've had the odd teething troubles, obviously, but generally I think we all agree it was a sound move.'

'We feel we're offering our patients a better service, and surely that's what counts?' Holly felt a faint rush of colour invade her cheeks as Sam's gaze swept over her, taking in the classic lines of her straight, knee-length skirt and the soft, jade-coloured silk shirt. 'As fund-holders we have more say in the type of treatment we can offer. To a certain extent the system is speeded up because we can shop around, so to speak. If one of our patients needs a hip replacement and the local hospital has a long waiting-list, we can try somewhere else. That has to be good.'

'You don't feel it might be creating a two-tier system, where fund-holders get precedence?'

She looked up sharply, expecting to see a cynical smile on his face, and was surprised to find that he was perfectly serious. She frowned. 'It isn't supposed to work like that.'

'But you suspect it might.'

Holly bit at her lower lip. 'We've taken what seems to be the best option for our practice. If we can get a better deal for the people in our care, then surely we have a responsibility to do so. Maybe you don't agree.'

'Hear, hear!' Betty nodded approval.

A faint smile twisted the corners of Sam's mouth. 'On the contrary, I'm all for anything that puts the patient first. It's good to know at the outset that I shall be working with a kindred spirit, especially,' he added softly, 'one who's prepared to come out fighting.'

The genuine note of pleasure and approval in his voice sent a tiny and thoroughly illogical *frisson* of happiness running through Holly, and she felt the tide of colour swim into her face as she sent him an answering smile. 'We do our best. This may be a fairly widespread rural community, but loyalties run deep.'

'Which brings me to another point.' Matt's empty pipe was in evidence again. He hadn't smoked for twelve months but habit died hard. 'We do a fair bit of our own casualty work. You'll have seen the treatment-room?'

Sam nodded. 'I'm impressed.'

'We thought long and hard about it and decided it wasn't a luxury, but something we needed. The nearest hospital casualty department is about twenty miles away. A lot of people prefer that we deal with their more minor surgery needs here.'

'What type of cases do you get?'

Kate looked at Matt, who nodded. 'Farm injuries, cut hands, legs, that sort of thing.' She grinned ruefully. 'It's a miracle we don't see more infected wounds. Obviously, they arrive in their working gear, probably having just mucked out the cows. I've seen some pretty nasty gashes covered in the most unspeakable gunge.'

'It must say a lot for the standard of care that you *don't* see more infection.'

'Well, at least we get to see and treat them more quickly than if they had to travel all the way to hospital and maybe sit around waiting in Casualty when they got there.'

'You did say you were prepared to undertake minor ops?' Matt queried.

'Glad to. Is there some sort of rota system?'

'Emergencies as and when, obviously.' Julie smiled. 'Whoever happens to be here at the time gets it. But any other non-urgent minor surgical procedures, such as removal of stitches, lancing of boils, is usually by appointment with the relevant doctor.'

'Sounds fair.'

'So. . .' Matt sat forward, placing his cup and saucer on the table. 'Anyone have any other problems?'

'Mr Hargreaves,' Holly put in.

'Old Jim Hargreaves?'

She nodded. 'His arthritis is affecting him pretty badly now. I went to see him a couple of days ago. He was in bed and really pretty close to the end of his tether. Walking's almost an impossibility now. It's not just his hip—the knee-joints are affected as well.'

Sam frowned. 'Have you tried getting him into hospital?'

She gave a wry smile. 'We've been trying for the past couple of years, but Jim has fought it all the way. It's not just that he's convinced that if he leaves the cottage he'll never go back—he was actually born there eighty-odd years ago—he's actually got a phobia about hospitals.'

'I take it you've had another talk with him?' Matt queried.

Holly nodded. 'He's still fighting against it, but even he knows he can't go on the way he is. Apart from anything else, he's not feeding himself properly.' She frowned. 'I'm going to ring the hospital at Fendale and have a word with Brian Connors, the consultant, and try to get Jim admitted as soon as possible, before he starts weakening again.'

'Good idea.'

Somewhere in the distance a phone started ringing. Julie groaned. 'Here we go. I'd better get that before the hordes start to descend.'

'Damn!' Matt looked at his watch. 'There are still a couple of points I needed to cover.'

'Do you still need me?' Kate was also on her feet. 'Only Mrs Thompson is due in at nine for her injection and I don't want to keep her hanging around—she's nervous enough as it is.'

'No, that's fine, you carry on.'

Holly was on her feet too, gathering up her briefcase. Sam placed the bundle of letters with exaggerated carefulness in her hands. 'Need any help?'

She flashed him a look. 'I think I can manage, thanks.' She heard his quiet rumble of laughter follow her as she made her way out.

An hour and a half later, Julie tapped at the door of the consulting-room and popped her head round. 'Sorry to bother you, but Mrs Calloway rang to cancel her ten-thirty appointment.'

Washing her hands, Holly returned to her desk and found the appropriate card. 'Right, well, that's one less anyway. Did she say why?'

'She thought she might have "a problem with her waterworks", as she put it, but it seems to have sorted itself out.'

Holly frowned. 'Did she bring in a urine specimen?'

'Yes. Kate checked it. Everything looks OK, but I told Mrs Calloway if she was at all worried to call in and make a new appointment.'

'That's fine.' Holly looked at her watch. 'Does that mean I've finished?'

'Ah, well, not quite. Mr Prescott called in on the off-chance. He's got a painful foot and wondered if you might take a look at it for him.'

'Right you are, send him in.' Frowning, Holly flipped through the pile of cards on her desk. 'Is it my imagination, or are we less busy than usual today?'

Julie chuckled. 'Put it down to the curiosity factor.'

'The curiosity factor?'

'They all want to see the new doctor, give him the once-over.'

'I see.' Holly briskly stacked a pile of journals on the shelf behind her desk. 'Well, let's hope they approve.'

'Oh, they do.' Laughter twinkled in Julie's brown eyes. 'According to Sharon Braithwaite, he's a bit of all right and the best thing that's happened round here for a long time.'

'Yes, well, as far as Sharon is concerned, anything in trousers is all right.'

'And Mrs Woolley reckons "he'll do".'

Holly raised an eyebrow. 'Praise, indeed. Let's hope it doesn't go to his head. And now,' she said briskly, 'shall we have Mr Prescott in and see if we can sort out his foot? Ah, Mr Prescott.' Smiling, she waved the hobbling forty-year-old to a chair beside her desk. 'You look decidedly uncomfortable. How long has the foot been bothering you? Look, slip your shoe and sock off so that I can take a look.'

'It's been a few days now.'

'Mmm.' Holly made a careful examination of the obviously swollen foot. 'It must be painful to walk on it?'

'Aye, it is that.' He grunted as she pressed the side of his big toe. 'It's swollen. I had trouble getting my shoe on this morning.'

'Yes, I can see. It feels hot, too. OK, George, you can pop your shoe back on now.' Straightening up,

Holly typed a few details on to the computer before looking at him. 'What you've got is gout.'

'Gout! Nay.' George Prescott was horrified. 'It can't be gout. I don't drink above a glass a week, and then I like a drop of ale. I never touch——'

'George.' Holly smiled reassuringly. 'I promise you, gout has nothing to do with the amount of alcohol you drink. That's an old wives' tale. Anyone can get gout. It's caused by a build-up of uric acid crystals in the joint.'

George looked relieved. 'Aye, well, thank God for that. If word got around as I'd been supping on the quiet. . . So, what can you do about it?'

'I can give you some tablets.' Holly tapped out the prescription, waited as it printed out, tore off the sheet of paper and signed it. 'These tablets will sort it out in no time. Take three a day and, if you get any more problems, come and see me, any time.'

Smiling, she watched him hobble out, and with a small sigh of pleasure turned her attention to the cooling cup of coffee Julie had left on her desk. Minutes later she walked through to Reception, depositing the bundle of record-cards and a folder of letters and forms on the desk in front of Betty.

'My contribution,' she smiled. 'Sorry you had to wait.'

'Well, let's hope everyone else gets the message.' Betty cocked her head meaningfully in the direction of the other doors. 'Naming no names, but some folk seem to think dealing with paperwork means filing it in the nearest waste-paper bin.'

Holly grinned. 'Talking of Uncle Matt, I don't suppose he's still here, is he?'

'No, sorry. He left shortly after the meeting.'

'How did he seem?'

'Tired. The man needs a good long holiday, but then there's no point saying it. Why? Was it important?'

'Well. . .no, not really. I just wanted to check dates. I'm due for another refresher session soon.'

Betty tutted disapprovingly as she reached under the desk for the diary. 'This new GP contract is all very well, but insisting that properly qualified doctors have to go back to school—because that's virtually what it is. . .'

Holly smiled slightly. 'It is only five lecture sessions. Anyway, it may be a bit inconvenient, but it's not a bad thing, and if that's what it takes to be able to claim reimbursement, it's not so bad. Let's see.' Holly flipped through the pages of the diary as the phone rang.

'Radleigh Medical Centre.' Betty tucked the receiver under her chin as she hunted for her pen, shifting papers and files. 'Yes, the doctor is still here.' She glanced up at Holly, who nodded. 'Yes. . .' Her face became serious. 'How old is he? No, no, you did the right thing, but I think you should let Doctor take a look at him.' She glanced up at the clock. 'We'll expect you in about five minutes, then.'

'What's the problem?'

'That was Mrs Drummond, from the junior school. One of the children has had a fall in the playground. It seems his leg is gashed quite badly. I said to bring him in straight away. It seemed more sensible than having to transport him all the way to hospital.'

'Is the treatment-room empty?' Holly was at once all professional.

'Yes, Kate finished her clinic about a quarter of an hour ago.'

'Good. I'll just make sure everything is ready. It sounds as though we may have a stitching job on our hands.'

Betty pulled a face. 'Poor little mite. Sooner you than me.'

'Did she give you the child's name?' Julie came in to scan the brief note Betty had scribbled down.

'Yes, it's young Jamie Clarke.'

'I might have known. I'll get his cards.'

Holly said, 'Have the parents been informed?'

'Mum's on her way.'

'Right, that sounds like a car now. Bring them straight through to the treatment-room.'

The patient, a freckle-faced eight-year-old, was clearly not happy. His tear-stained face belied the tough-guy image of his crew-cut hair. One muddy training-shoe dangled from his fist as he was carried into the surgery by a harassed-looking young teacher.

'Bring him through here.' Holly smiled. 'I'll just get this cleaned up a bit, so that I can take a proper look. That's right, up on the couch. Oh, yes.' She studied the fairly deep and none too clean gash just below the knee.

'I want me mam.'

'She's on her way. I'm sure she'll be here any minute now.' Holly frowned. 'You certainly made a good job of this, didn't you?'

'They were playing commandos in the playground. We have a small wooded conservation area set aside in the school grounds,' Harriet Briggs explained defensively. 'It's used for nature lessons. The children know they aren't allowed there at any other time. They're always supervised at playtime but. . .well, you just can't watch them all of the time. Jamie was up a tree.'

'Ow! O...w! Ouch!' howled the victim, clutching at his leg and thrusting away Holly's hand as she gently tried to swab away some of the mud and blood from the site of the injury.

'I'm afraid I have to try to clean away some of this

dirt, so that I can see how much damage you've done. I promise I'll try not to hurt.'

'Geroff! Ouch! I want me mam.'

Holly turned away, reaching for a fresh swab. 'It's not too bad,' she confided quietly to the anxious young teacher. 'I'm afraid it might need a couple of stitches.'

The girl swallowed hard, her face paling visibly. 'I can't. . . I don't think. . .'

'Look, there's really no need for you to watch. Why don't you sit in the waiting-room?' Holly advised gently. 'You can keep a look-out for his mum and let her know what's happened.'

'Good idea. She's bound to be worried.'

Holly forced a smile and, drawing a deep breath, returned her attention to her patient. Tears trickled down his cheeks. A grubby fist dashed them away. 'I ain't having no stitches, you can't make me.' A small clenched fist made sharp contact with Holly's cheekbone, bringing tears to her eyes, then a foot was aimed at her stomach.

Winded, she gasped, closing her eyes for a few seconds as she leaned heavily against the couch, waiting for a wave of nausea to pass.

'Need any help?' A voice spoke quietly from the open doorway.

She opened her eyes and felt an illogical surge of relief run through her as Sam walked into the room. 'I think I'm quite glad to see you.' She gave a tight smile.

A spasm flickered across his features, leaving them taut as he moved closer, supporting her with a hand beneath her arm. 'Are you all right?'

'Fi-fine, I think.' Or at least she would be, once she got her breath back.

He peered at the bloodied leg. 'What do we have here, then? My word, that's pretty impressive. A war-wound, from the look of it.'

It was fascinating, and just a little galling, to see young Jamie's tears disappear as if by magic. Rubbing the back of a grubby hand across his nose, he leaned back, offering the injured limb for inspection.

'I fell out of a tree,' he announced proudly. 'We was watchin' for the enemy.'

'And I'll bet you gave them what-for.' Talking gently, Sam applied a swab and scrutinised the wound. Holly watched in disbelief as he cleaned away the blood, leaving the gash exposed but at least clean. 'How many casualties did you have?' Sam enquired gravely.

'Just me and Ginger.' A loud sniff accompanied the report. 'But 'e only 'ad a scratch. It didn't even need a plaster.'

Sam's dark brows drew together. 'Well, I think this is probably going to need a plaster. A very large one— don't you think, Dr Palmer?—for a wound like this.'

Stifling a tiny and what she knew was a totally illogical feeling of resentment, Holly lowered her voice as Sam deliberately led her away from the examination couch. 'Ideally it could do with a couple of stitches, but I don't think he's going to let anyone try. At least he had an anti-tetanus jab fairly recently, according to his records.'

Why, she wondered, did she suddenly feel like a raw probationer in medical school, explaining her actions— or rather, lack of them? 'I suppose we could try steri-strips. They'll probably hold the edges of the skin in place long enough for it to start healing. It's worth a try, anyway.'

Sam grinned. 'And a large dressing to keep them in place—large enough to impress his friends.'

'I'd better see to it.' There was the sound of a commotion from the reception desk. Holly sighed, brushing a hand against her aching cheekbone. 'That's probably the mother. She sounds pretty hysterical. That's all I need.'

Sam looked at her, his mouth tightening briefly. 'Look, can you cope here? I'll head her off if you like. At least it will give you a breathing-space. Or would you rather I took over?'

She stiffened defensively. 'I think I can manage, thank you.' Maybe not as brilliantly as he would have done, but she wasn't about to let herself be defeated by an eight-year-old.

Gently probing what would inevitably be a bruise on her cheek, she emerged from the treatment-room some five minutes later with her patient, now proudly sporting a limp and an extra-large dressing on his knee.

Sam was smiling at an anxious-faced young woman, probably in her late twenties, petite, attractive, and with the kind of thick blonde hair Holly had always secretly envied. Seeing them together, she felt an unreasoned twist of emotion which, she told herself, couldn't possibly be jealousy.

'There we are.' Sam turned, grinning, as young Jamie flung himself in the direction of his mother. 'What did I tell you? He's as right as rain. A little bruised and battered, but he'll live to fight another day.'

'Jamie, what have you been up to? Oh, I'm so grateful, Doctor.' Blue eyes passed, smiling, but with polite uninterest, over Holly. 'I was so worried, I can't tell you.'

'Don't worry about it,' Sam said soothingly. 'It's all part of the service, any time. It's what we're here for. Isn't that right, Dr Palmer?'

Holly almost choked. The man was insufferable as well as arrogant. Flinging him a look of disgust, she gathered up her briefcase and headed for the door. 'Yes, well, I can see you don't need me.' She smiled sweetly, wincing as the darkening bruise made its presence felt. 'You obviously have things nicely under control here, so I'll leave you to it.'

Hunched into her jacket, she turned the collar up and marched out into the snow. All part of the service, indeed! At this rate, patients would be queuing up at the doors, waiting to get in just to see Dr Charm!

She climbed into the car, grated the gears and swore under her breath, all too aware of the figure reflected in the driving-mirror as she drove away.

The arrogance of the man! She was suddenly aware that her hands were gripping the steering-wheel much too tightly, and she forced herself to relax. Without as much as a by-your-leave, he had come striding in and more or less taken charge of *her* patient. At this rate, before she knew it, he'd probably have taken over the entire practice.

It was galling to discover that he was only seconds behind her when she drew up outside the cottage. She purposely ignored him, slamming the car door to a close, fumbling with her keys and heading for her own front door.

'Holly, wait!'

She resolutely ignored him. Her face hurt, her stomach hurt, and right now he was the last person in the world she wanted to see.

Her foot slipped on a patch of ice. Sam's hand shot out to steady her. She tried to pull away, but his grip firmed and she was shaken by the feeling of warmth and strength that seemed to run through her.

'I need to talk to you.'

'There's nothing to say. I'm tired. Please get out of my way.'

He studied her, taking in the firm set of her mouth, the truculence in the taut angle of her jaw. 'I've upset you.'

'Upset!' Her head jerked up and she gave a short laugh. 'Contrary to what you may believe, Dr Stratton, you don't yet run this practice. If I need help, I'll ask for it.'

His gaze narrowed. He stared down at her, his face taut. 'I'm sorry. I thought you needed help.'

'Yes, well, you were wrong. Still, I'm sure your efforts didn't go unrewarded,' she snapped uncharitably, and felt the breath catch in her throat as Sam's eyes glinted dangerously.

'I'm sorry if I've done anything to upset you. I simply did what I thought was for the best.' His thumb brushed against her cheek. 'That's going to be a nasty bruise. Holly, I'm sorry.'

Confused, she lifted her face involuntarily to his. Their breath fanned white into the cold air. Why couldn't he just leave her alone? What was it about this man that she only had to be near him for the alarm bells to start ringing inside her head?

Juggling with her keys, she tried to insert one in the lock. His hand came down over hers, preventing it, making no attempt to let her go. She swallowed hard, feeling suddenly ridiculously vulnerable. She closed her eyes briefly and shook her head. 'No, *I'm* sorry. It wasn't your fault. I'm the one who should be apologising. I made a mess of things. Let's just leave it at that, shall we? Put it down to a lousy day.' She tried to turn away but his hands were on her shoulders, forcing her to face him.

'I'd like to think we could, but somehow I get the feeling it's never going to be that easy,' he said softly. 'I don't want us to be enemies, Holly.'

She looked into the taut features and felt a tremor of something closely akin to excitement run through her. The sensuous mouth was only a breath away. Her lips parted on a gasp as he suddenly pulled her towards his powerfully male body, bringing her so close that her nostrils were invaded by the clean, musky smell of him.

Shock briefly widened her eyes as, almost negligently, his finger traced the curve of her cheek. She shook her head as, slowly, he bent his head and kissed her firmly on the mouth.

She stood mesmerised, stunned by the power of the sensations that coursed through her. Moaning softly, she swayed towards him. His grip tightened, sending a tingling awareness of him surging through her. It was like nothing she had ever experienced before. Even when Martin had kissed her, it had never been quite like this. She didn't want to be his enemy, either. That was the trouble—she didn't know what she did want, but she certainly wasn't ready for what was happening.

The thought hit her like a shock-wave and suddenly she was struggling to break free. What on earth was she thinking of? She didn't even like the man. Worse than that, she didn't trust him. She pushed him away firmly. 'Please, let me go.'

He released her instantly, breathing hard. Blue eyes glinted. 'I thought we'd agreed to be friends.'

'Friends!' She almost choked on the word. 'Don't push your luck, Dr Stratton.' She inserted the key firmly into the lock and turned it. 'We may have to work together, we may even have to be neighbours, but there's no law says I have to like you. This is for Uncle Matt's sake. I suggest you remember that in future.' Gathering up her briefcase, she opened the door and put herself firmly on the other side of it, but not before an odd sound, which might have been a cough or could have been a chuckle, followed her.

She didn't stop to find out. Sam Stratton was an unsettling influence, one she could well do without. She preferred her life the way it was, thank you very much: quiet, maybe even vaguely boring, but uncomplicated and definitely safe.

CHAPTER FOUR

'IF YOU'VE got any sense at all, you'll stay right where you are today,' Holly admonished Thomas, who faced her with a look of feline contempt before stretching out full length on the chair and proceeding to wash his fur. 'I see. Well, be like that, see if I care.'

Grinning, Holly collected her mobile phone from the table, tickled the cat under his chin, checked his water-dish and turned off the radio. 'See you later, Tank. Oh, and don't go visiting the neighbour. He may look nice, but appearances can be very deceptive. Take my word.'

Glancing out of the window, she shuddered, reaching for her jacket and slipping it on over her neat black ski-pants and long sweater. Fresh overnight snow had renewed the white blanket covering fields and hedge-rows, giving them a picture-postcard beauty, but which, she knew, was going to make life more difficult. Still, at least the coast was clear.

Almost a week of trying to avoid seeing Sam had gone some way to restoring her confidence, although she was well aware that was merely postponing the inevitable. But at least this way, when they did eventually meet, she would be more composed, better prepared.

She saw the postman coming down the path and waved. Seconds later a pile of letters plopped on to the mat. Nibbling on the cold remains of a piece of toast, she flipped through them.

'Three brown envelopes—that means bills. Yeuk! One medical journal, two junk mail—and you know where you belong.' Her foot depressed the pedal on the waste-bin and she dropped the unopened envelopes inside. 'And one from——' her gaze fell on the Australian stamp '—Mum. Great.' She felt a momentary pang of sadness, then grinned and propped the airmail letter against a plant-pot on the table. 'I'll save you for later—my special treat.'

A glance at the clock sent her heading for the door. Hesitating, she looked out at the virgin snow. 'Coast still clear,' she muttered, and made a dash for her car, sweeping a layer of snow from the bonnet and windscreen.

Her key turned in the ignition. Nothing happened. She stared at the dashboard in disbelief and tried again, with the same result. 'Come *on*.' Her hand beat against the steering-wheel in frustration. 'Don't do this to me.' She turned the key again, flung open the door and climbed out to lift the bonnet, peering inside with a look of disgust. 'Why do you do this?' she muttered. 'Don't I keep you fed and watered? Aren't I nice to you?'

'Having trouble?' The quiet drawl came from behind her.

She jerked upwards, cracking her head on the bonnet, and let out a yelp of mingled pain and frustration. 'Do you have to creep up on people like that?'

'I wasn't creeping,' Sam said evenly. 'You were so busy talking to yourself, you didn't hear.' He peered over her shoulder. 'Were you looking for something in particular?'

'How would I know?' She threw him a malevolent look as she nursed a tender spot on her scalp. 'People always look under the bonnet when a car won't start. I assumed there must be a reason.'

A glint of mischief lit his dark eyes. 'I think you'll find that only applies if there's a problem with the engine.'

'And I suppose——' she managed with an effort to keep her voice very cool '—you know what's wrong?'

The smell of expensive aftershave drifted into her nostrils. Dressed in a dark suit, the material stretched taut against the hard muscles of his thighs, Sam looked powerfully masculine. The blue eyes glinted. 'Oh, I know exactly what your problem is.'

'You—you do?'

'Absolutely.' He reached out a muscular arm. She stiffened, feeling the breath catch in her throat. A glimmer of amusement flickered in his eyes before he slammed the car's bonnet neatly back into place, making her jump. 'You have a flat battery. Naughty, naughty, Dr Palmer. I'm surprised at you.'

Colour flared defensively in her cheeks. She swallowed hard. 'Can—can it be fixed?'

'That depends. Do you have any leads?'

'Leads?'

'Jump-leads.'

'No,' she said flatly.

'Pity. We could have run them from my car to start yours. As it is, you'll have to get in touch with the breakdown services or the garage and get them to send someone out to fix it.'

She stared at him in dismay. 'But that could take hours.'

'Probably.' He looked at his watch. 'At this rate we're both going to be late. You'd better come in with me and phone from the surgery.'

Easing herself into the passenger seat, Holly sat in silence, gazing out of the window until he had manoeuvred out of the narrow lane. The car's heater was efficient, which was more than could be said for her own. She acknowledged guiltily that her resolution to do something about changing the fairly ancient model was long overdue.

She found herself surreptitiously studying Sam's profile, as if it might tell her what was going on behind those enigmatic features.

'I'm sorry about this,' she offered. 'It was stupid of me to let the battery go flat. . .'

'Forget it.' He didn't disturb his concentration by turning to look at her, but she saw the fractional movement of his brows. 'As a matter of fact, I'm glad of a chance to speak to you. I don't seem to have had much of an opportunity lately.'

He looked directly at her this time and her chin lifted. 'I've been busy. More calls because of the weather—you know what it's like. The more elderly patients can't get to the surgery.'

'You don't have to explain. I simply wanted to ask if you remember a patient by the name of Waring?'

She frowned. 'Waring. Waring. No. . . Oh, wait, yes. Seventy-ish, lives alone.'

'Widowed.' Sam nodded, concentrating on the road again as they approached the outskirts of the town. 'Husband died about nine months ago.'

'Fran Waring.'

'That's the one.' He signalled and overtook a school bus which was labouring up the hill. 'How well do you know her?'

She gave a slight laugh. 'Probably as well as anyone could know Fran, I suppose. She likes her own company, does Fran. Independent as they come. God knows how she survives in that old barn of a place.'

'I know what you mean.'

Holly looked at him, seeing the attractive features briefly relaxed by a smile. 'Why, is there a problem?'

'I think there might be.' Sam frowned. 'I had a call a couple of days ago, from the niece.'

'Niece?' Surprised, Holly turned to look at him. 'I

didn't think Fran had any relatives, at least none living locally.'

'I doubt if many people did.' They reached the small car park adjoining the practice. He parked and switched off the ignition without making any attempt to move. 'I gather the niece was making one of her sporadic visits and felt sufficiently concerned about her aunt to call the surgery and ask me to pay a visit.'

'Is there a specific problem? I mean, Fran's always been a pretty tough old bird. I doubt if she's taken as much as an asprin all her life.'

A half-smile tugged at his lips. 'I rather got that impression.'

Holly laughed. 'I take it she wasn't too pleased to see you?'

'You can say that again.'

'So why the call?' Her troubled gaze levelled with his.

'The niece said her aunt had a cough, which is true, but I get the feeling that time is starting to catch up with Fran. You know her. How long is it since you last saw her?'

Holly frowned, tucking a stray wisp of hair behind her ear. 'Well, actually she was more Uncle Matt's patient than mine, although I did go out—what?— probably about six months ago. It was his day off. Fran had taken a bit of a tumble.' She screwed up her face, trying to remember. 'As far as I recall, nothing was broken. She wouldn't go to hospital for an X-ray so I strapped the wrist up for her and got the district nurse to pop in.' Again a half-smile curved her lips. 'I don't think she got beyond the front door. Uncle Matt saw her a couple of weeks later, by which time Fran had taken the strapping off, anyway, and she was carrying on as normal. 'Why?'

Sam's mouth tightened fractionally. 'It seems she's taken to going for walks.'

'So what's wrong with that? Lots of people do.'

'Not in the middle of the night.'

'Ah, I see.'

'And the niece is afraid her aunt isn't eating properly.'

'Do you think she's right?'

'Could be.' Sam frowned. 'I'd not seen her before, but in my estimation she is definately underweight.'

'So what are you going to do?'

'I'll be seeing her again, obviously. In the meantime, the niece has arranged to stop over for a few days. I just wanted to get some background from you.'

'I hope it helps.'

'I'm sure it will.'

She climbed out of the car. Sam slammed his door and came round, reaching past her as she fumbled for her briefcase.

'Here, let me.' As he did so his hand brushed against her arm, sending a momentary shock-wave running through her. He was so close that she could see the firm texture of his skin. No matter how much she might dislike Sam Stratton's arrogance, there was no denying that he possessed an animal magnetism. She straightened up, alarmed by the direction her thoughts had suddenly taken.

She swallowed hard and smiled. 'Thanks again for the lift. I'm very grateful. If you hadn't——'

'I told you to forget it,' he said evenly, and looked at his watch. 'Anyway, I have to go. Duty calls. I'll probably see you later.'

She stood in the snow, watching him stride away, and felt the warm colour invade her cheeks. Blast the man, she thought with a rare sense of irritation. He was behaving as if that kiss had never happened. Deep down, she knew she should be pleased, instead of which, perversely, she felt cheated.

It was a busy morning with a steady stream of patients coming and going. Winter brought requests for flu jabs, and the inevitable rise in cases of bronchitis, as well as an increase in the number of injuries caused by falls.

As a patient left, Julie brought in another batch of cards. 'Sorry. These are the last—with appointments, anyway. Would you like me to bring you a coffee?'

Holly flicked through the pile and shook her head. 'Better not. I'll press on. I'm sure everyone would like to get home. I can't say I blame them. Who's next?'

'Mr Page.'

'Right, send him in, then. Mr Page.' Holly smiled, rising to her feet as the man shuffled into the consulting-room. 'Oh, dear. Can you sit down?'

'It's the back, Doctor.' Mike Page grunted. He looked at the chair and shook his head. 'I don't think I can make it.'

'How did it happen? You just stand still. If you can, loosen your shirt so that I can examine your back. Yes, that's fine.'

'I was cleaning the car, bent down to pick up the sponge and. . .' He grimaced as Holly gently probed the painful area. 'Yes, that's it.'

'Can you lean forward, slowly?' She watched as he attempted it. 'That's fine. . . No, don't push it. You can tuck your shirt in again.' Returning to the desk, Holly glanced at her computer notes. 'I see you had the same problem about twelve months ago. Let me see, what did we give you then?'

'Tablets—can't remember what they were. Anti-inflammatory, or something.'

'That's right. I've found it. How did you get on with them?'

He pulled a face. 'Not too bad. They made me feel sick.'

Holly frowned. 'Yes, I'm afraid that can happen sometimes.' She tapped out a prescription. 'We'll try you with something different—capsules this time. You take just one a day. They have a time-release action. I think you'll find they do the trick, but, if not, come back and see me again.'

The door closed on the last of the morning's patients. Holly dictated a couple of letters of referral to consultants at the local hospital and extracted the cassette from the machine, carrying it with the record-cards and depositing them on the desk in Reception.

'Morning, Doctor.'

Smiling, she looked up. 'Morning, Joe, and how's old Moss here?' She bent to fondle the elderly collie. 'You're a nice fellow, aren't you?' Frowning, she straightened up. 'Did you need to see me, Joe? Surgery is finished but I could——'

'No, don't fret yourself. I've just been down to collect my pension and thought I'd kill two birds with one stone and pop in for a repeat prescription for my blood-pressure pills, that's all.'

'Have you seen the nurse?'

'Oh, aye, she's checked it and says it's the same as usual.'

'Right, well, in that case. . .' Holly rummaged in a wire tray on the desk. 'Yes, here it is. I remember now, I signed it earlier.' She handed the prescription over and looked down at the dog stretched out at the man's feet. 'Moss must be getting on a bit now?'

'Aye, same as me.' The pensioner grinned. 'We takes our time, but we gets there sooner or later.'

'I'm sure he must be good company for you.'

'I don't know what I'd do without him, right enough.

He's not hearing so well these days, but he's happy enough. Come on then, lad, let's be away.'

Smiling, Holly watched the pair amble out.

Julie replaced the phone, put up the 'Surgery closed' sign and nodded in the direction of the nearest consulting-room. 'I thought you'd want to know, your uncle is in again.'

'Oh, no.'

'He was catching up on some paperwork when I went in about five minutes ago.'

Holly bit back a sigh. 'I'd better go and have a quick word with him before I go out.' She shook her head. 'I don't know what I'm going to do with him. I can't physically keep him away from the surgery.'

Julie gave a wry smile. 'He's a stubborn man. I think you're fighting a losing battle.'

'That's the trouble. If he doesn't listen to reason, I'm afraid he's going to do some real damage. Oh, well, I'll try to talk some sense into him. Oh, by the way, are you sure you don't mind loaning me your car for a couple of hours?'

'Feel free. The baby clinic is still going strong, so I'm stuck here anyway.' Julie brushed a hand against her forehead as she reached into her bag and handed over the keys.

'You're an angel. I've had a word with the garage and they'll deliver mine back to the cottage tonight.' She paused, frowning, to study the girl. 'Are you all right? You look a bit peaky.'

Julie gave a slight laugh. 'Who, me? Yes, I'm fine. Bit of a cold, that's all.'

'Well, if you're sure. I'll see you later.'

Tapping at the door of Matthew Wainwright's consulting-room, she popped her head round in response to his command to enter. 'Busy?' she asked pointedly.

'No, just finished. Come in.' He popped a tablet into

his mouth, returning the bottle hastily to his pocket. His face had a greyish tinge to it. Holly studied him dispassionately and felt a shiver of anxiety run through her.

'Uncle Matt, are you still having problems with indigestion?'

He rose to his feet, patting her arm. 'It's much better. I'm fine, just the odd twinge every now and again. Nothing to worry about. So, what can I do for you, then?'

She accepted the reassurance, knowing it was what he wished, but resolved silently to keep an eye on him. 'I wondered whether you'd heard anything from the hospital about young Lucy Benson?'

He frowned, sifting through a mass of paperwork on his desk. 'Funny you should ask. The report came through this morning, as a matter of fact.' He handed it to her. 'It's not the best news, I'm afraid.'

Holly scanned the report and looked at him. 'Leukaemia.'

'Pretty much what we expected.'

She swallowed hard. 'It's going to be hard on the family, even though I think they suspected the worst. Still, at least now they'll know what they're facing and, funnily enough, in a strange sort of way, that can make things easier—for some people, anyway. I presume she'll be starting a course of treatment straight away?'

Matthew Wainwright nodded. 'At least we can offer hope, which I couldn't have done a few years ago. These days, thank God, childhood leukaemia has about an eighty per cent chance of recovery, and they're a close family, which helps.' He looked at his watch. 'Well, I'm off. Just thought I'd clear up a few things.' He reached for his jacket and her previous worries were strengthened as he shrugged himself, with an effort, into it.

He looked tired. Worse than that, he looked exhausted, which made it all the more galling when she had to admit to herself that Sam was right. No amount of persuasion, gentle or otherwise, was going to make the older man change the habits of a lifetime. The life of an invalid would hold no charms for a man who had been as active as he had.

'Time I was off, too.' Her throat tightened as she followed him out. She was about to head for the car when Sam appeared in the corridor that linked the individual consulting-rooms. Deep in her own thoughts, she gave him a remote smile and turned away.

'Holly, I need to talk to you.' His jacket was unfastened, to reveal a blue shirt. His gaze narrowed. 'Are you all right?'

'What?' She blinked hard. 'Oh, yes, I'm fine. What can I do for you?'

'If I've picked a bad time. . .'

'No.' She shook her head. 'It's fine.'

'I'm going out to see Fran Waring later this afternoon. I was hoping you might go with me.'

'Me?'

'You know her. Somehow or other I have to make her see that she can't go on as she is. Ideally she'd be better off living with her niece, or someone who can give her the care she needs, but she's already rejected that idea out of hand.'

'Are you sure the niece would have her?'

'She says so.' Sam ran a hand through his dark hair. 'Which leaves a couple of alternatives. Either warden-controlled accommodation, where she can retain her independence but have the security of knowing someone is on call, or we have to persuade her to accept more help.'

Holly gave a wry smile. 'I don't much fancy your chances.'

'Nor do I, which is why I need you with me. I think she might listen to you. At the very least, you can back up my arguments.'

'I have a couple of calls to make.'

'So have I. Suppose I pick you up later?'

Which he did. It was mid-afternoon by the time she slid into the passenger seat beside him. As they headed along the narrow lanes she studied him unhappily.

'I hope you realise I'm doing this against my better judgement.'

'I'm grateful.' He took his eyes off the road long enough to glance at her.

'Don't be,' she warned. 'I agreed to come along to give some moral support. I'm still not convinced I can do anything to help. If Fran decides to stay where she is, nothing will shift her and I won't see her bullied.'

A spasm flickered briefly across his face. 'Whatever else you may think of me, Holly, I'm not a bully. I'm all for elderly people retaining their independence. In Fran's case, I just want to be sure she can do it safely.' His dark brows drew together. 'I'd be failing in my duty if I did nothing and she had another accident or died from simple neglect—surely you can see that?'

She bit her lip and was still pondering the problem when they reached the farmhouse a few minutes later.

Fran's niece led them into the small sitting-room. A log fire crackled in the hearth. A single lamp cast a small patch of brightness into the early darkness of the afternoon.

'How is she?' Sam asked.

'Not so good, really. She's dozing,' Jill Waring said quietly, picking up a cup from the small table. 'I made her a spot of lunch but she only picked at it. Auntie, it's the doctor come to see you.'

Holly looked at the woman sleeping in the chair and felt a tiny ripple of shock run through her. Fran somehow seemed smaller, more vulnerable than when she had last seen her. Always tall and surprisingly strong after an active life, Fran had suddenly, overnight it seemed, become a tiny, frail old woman.

Sam put his briefcase on the floor. Sitting in the chair opposite, he gently reached out to hold one small blue-veined hand, his fingers registering the rapid pulse. 'Fran, can you hear me? it's Dr Stratton. I said I'd call in to see you again, do you remember?' He smiled as the paper-thin lids flickered open.

'Albert, is that you?' Fran blinked. 'I didn't hear you come in.'

'You were having a little doze,' Sam grinned. 'I don't blame you. That's a grand fire you have there.'

Fran sat up. 'You're home early. I haven't got your tea. . .'

'Now, don't you worry about it.' Sam pressed a hand gently, over hers, throwing a questioning glance at Jill Waring.

The younger woman's eyes filled with tears. 'She thinks you're my Uncle Albert. He died ten years ago.'

Sam nodded, his expression betraying nothing as he held Fran's hands. 'Fran, do you remember me? I'm Dr Stratton. I called to see you a few days ago. You were feeling a bit poorly. And this is Holly.' He beckoned her forward. 'You know Dr Palmer.'

Holly smiled. 'Hello, Fran. How are you feeling? I hear you've not been too well.'

Blue eyes clouded with confusion. 'I've had a bit of a cough.'

'Yes, that's right. Dr Stratton gave you some medicine. Are you feeling better?'

'Albert will be wanting his tea. I've made a bit of cake. . .'

'Albert isn't here, Fran,' Sam said, gently. 'Do you know what day it is Fran? Can you remember?'

The watery eyes gazed at him.

'Don't worry about it, Fran, it's not important. Now, I just want to listen to your chest,' Sam said. 'Is that all right?' He took the stethoscope Holly held out and she watched as he made his examination, the strong hands moving with surprising gentleness until he straightened up.

'You've still got a bit of a rattle in there, haven't you? I really think you need to go into hospital for a while, just to get you sorted out.'

'I don't want to go into hospital. Why should I go? I'll be all right here, with Albert. He'll look after me.'

'Don't worry about it,' Sam said gently. He looked at Holly, and she bent to put an arm round the thin frame.

'You really need to get that cough sorted out, Fran. It's making you feel poorly and you're not eating properly.'

'I'm not hungry. I don't want to eat.'

'No, I know you don't, but you do need someone to look after you for a while, until you feel better. I promise you, as soon as you're well enough, you can come home again.'

Sam shot a look in her direction, nodding almost imperceptibly towards the door.

'You're not happy about her, are you?'

He lowered his voice as they moved away fractionally. 'I think she's got an infection bubbling away in there, and she's certainly confused.'

'That could be down to the temperature—in part, anyway.' Holly looked up at him. 'What do you want to do?'

'Get her admitted to the general hospital, to start with, anyway. They'll be able to keep an eye on her while they treat the infection.'

'What about after that?' Jill Waring asked anxiously

as she joined them. 'I'd stay with her, but I've got the family. Tom's managing, but he's got his work, and the kids have to get to school. . .'

'There's nothing you could do, anyway,' Sam said gently. 'At the moment my first concern is the chest infection.'

'It's serious, isn't it?'

'It could be. Your aunt isn't young, and physically she's very run-down. If I can get her to hospital, they'll be able to assess her condition.'

'It's pretty obvious she can't cope alone here, not in her present state, anyway,' Holly agreed.

'Obviously, if she doesn't improve, we'd have to think of moving her to the local geriatric hospital, on a short-term basis, anyway.'

'She's not going to be happy about it.'

'No, I realise that.' Sam frowned. 'But I honestly don't think we have any choice.'

Jill Waring looked at him. 'What are her chances of coming back here?'

'I'd be lying if I said I could guarantee it. A lot depends on your aunt herself. She's always been pretty strong, I gather. She's determined. If we can sort out the infection, her mental state could improve too. In which case, given the proper support, which we can arrange, there's every possibility she can return home. The critical factor is the next few days. If we can get over that, I'd say we can be more positive about the future.'

'I'll sort out some clothes and a few things to take with her.' Jill Waring headed for the stairs.

Holly said, 'Would you like me to get on to the ambulance people?'

'You'll have to use the mobile phone. Holly?' Turning, she almost collided in the doorway with his solid, muscular frame. He stared down at her and, before she knew what was happening, his mouth came down to brush against hers and she found herself holding her breath as a strange new sense of awareness brought the faint colour to her cheeks. 'I'm glad you came with me. Thanks.'

She watched him stride away before she turned and hurried out into the early darkness, glad of the biting wind that cooled her cheeks.

It was almost an hour later and completely dark before the ambulance was finally on its way and they made their way back to the cottage.

Climbing into the passenger seat, Holly leaned her head back, closing her eyes, feeling suddenly very weary. Sam drove in silence for a while and she was glad. Her head seemed to be spinning. Lack of food, probably, she silently chided herself. But it was more than that, she knew. It was a combination of things: sadness for Fran, concern for Uncle Matt, and a sudden, disturbing awareness of her own vulnerability where Sam was concerned.

In the darkness she watched as he drove. She had been moved by his patience, both with the child last week, and then with Fran. Not every doctor would have spent an hour of his valuable time trying to persuade an elderly lady to place her life in his hands.

Such strong, capable hands. Memories of their force-fulness as he had drawn her towards him and kissed her sent an involuntary flush of anticipation running through her and she had to drag herself back to reality, stifling a sigh.

'Are you all right?' Sam turned his head to glance in her direction.

She nodded, reluctant to open her eyes but suddenly, illogically, very glad to have him there. 'Tired, that's all. Heaven knows why. You did all the work.'

'Reaction, it's natural. She is in the best place, you know.'

Holly nodded. 'That's what I keep telling myself.'

As they reached the cottage he brought the car to a halt, cutting the ignition but making no attempt to get out. 'There wasn't any other alternative. You do see that? Fran couldn't have coped in that place alone. What if she'd had an accident?'

'You don't have to explain. I know it was the logical thing to do, but that doesn't make it any easier.' She looked at him. 'It came as a shock, seeing her that way. She's always been so active, so full of life.'

'Right now she's a sick old lady, Holly.' He was so close that his arm, along the seat behind her, brushed against her hair.

'It all seems so unfair.'

'It happens. We're doctors; we're human. We can't turn back the clock, perform miracles.' His hand was on her shoulder, gently forcing her to look at him. He caught the glint of tears in her eyes. She heard him swear softly, then she was fumbling frantically with the seatbelt and climbing out.

He was beside her before she could gather her things, holding her when she would have broken away. 'Holly, what is it?'

'Nothing. Everything. I don't know.' She ran a hand distractedly through her hair. 'It was seeing Fran. She'd changed so much in such a short time.'

His gaze narrowed. 'You must have seen it happen before, with other patients?'

'Yes, of course I have,' she bit out. 'Seeing Fran just brought it all home to me, that's all.' She broke off as, from inside the cottage, the phone began to ring. With a small sigh of exasperation she fumbled in her bag for the key, inserted it in the lock and, without pausing to close the door or to switch on the light, hurried to answer it.

'Yes, Dr Palmer speaking. Mrs Cooper? No, that's fine, any time. Yes, of course I remember. In what way worried? Yes, unfortunately the antibiotics are going to take some time to work. Katy has quite a bad throat infection so she's probably going to feel quite poorly for a day or so. You can give her a dose of Calpol—that should bring her temperature down. Yes. . . If it doesn't and you're still worried, call me again. Not at all. Any time.'

Replacing the receiver, pausing to scribble a note on the pad, she half turned. 'I'm sorry about that, I——' She broke off on the realisation that she was talking to herself. The room was empty.

For the first time in a long time, a sudden feeling of loneliness swept over her, threatening to overwhelm her in its intensity. She stood gazing into the semi-darkness of the room and felt a sense of disappointment run through her.

So what did you expect? What did you imagine? she chided herself. Did you think he was going to follow? So what if he had? What then? You don't need complications in your life, remember?

Swallowing hard on the tightness in her throat, she straightened up, tossing her jacket on to a chair, and made her way into the kitchen. What you need, my girl, she told herself briskly, is a long soak in a hot bath and an early night. At least she wasn't on emergency call.

Pushing open the door, she came to an abrupt halt, blinking as the glare of the light hit her. She gasped as Sam turned and held out a cup.

'Coffee? I took the liberty.'

She stared at him, suddenly not knowing whether to

laugh or cry, confused by a welter of emotions she was trying desperately hard not to acknowledge.

'I thought we could both use some.' He spooned sugar into her cup and she stared at him, wishing she hadn't as her eyes encountered his mouth, firm and attractive and far too much of a threat to her peace of mind right now.

'I—I thought you'd gone.'

'I don't walk away from unfinished business, Holly.' He drained his own coffee, set the cup down, in the process glancing briefly at the letter she had left on the kitchen table earlier that morning. He raised an eyebrow. 'Australia?'

She couldn't help smiling at his imitation of the accent. 'My mother. I told you she remarried. Doug is Australian.'

'You must miss her.'

'It's not so bad. We write often and talk on the phone.' She frowned. 'Obviously, right now, she's worried about Uncle Matt.'

'And what about you?' Sam prompted softly. 'Are you still worried?'

'Of course I am. How could I not be? Did you know that he was at the surgery again this morning? *Working*! He of all people should know what sort of chance he's taking, yet he behaves as if he knows better than the doctors. Or. . .' She bit at her lower lip as she looked up at him. 'Or maybe he doesn't trust me to keep things going. . .'

'Hey, come on. That's crazy and you know it.' His hands closed over her arms. 'You're tired and over-reacting, that's all.'

'You didn't see him.' She strained backwards, trying to push him away. Frustratingly his grasp merely tightened, sending a tingling surge of awareness running through her. She resisted it. Right now she needed a clear head. 'He was taking a tablet. Oh, he tried to hide it. I just happened to walk in at the wrong moment. I saw his face. He looked ill.'

'What do you want to do, Holly? You can't wrap him in cotton wool. Medicine is his life. He can't just press a switch and shut it off.'

'You think I don't know that?' She began to struggle, and her face flamed as her body made sharp contact with his. For a second, panic widened her eyes as the sheer physical awareness of his body surged through her. 'What is it to you, anyway? Uncle Matt means nothing to you.'

'I respect him, as a man and professionally. As far as Matt is concerned I'm here for a few weeks.'

She stared at him. 'I don't understand. So what are you saying?'

'I'm saying we can't make him change the habits of a lifetime. He knows the risks. I've seen other cases like Matt.' His mouth tightened grimly.

Suddenly her mouth felt dry. 'What—what are you trying to tell me? Sam, I have a right to know.'

His gaze narrowed. 'The attack was worse than he admits. I checked his medical records. Maybe I shouldn't have. He could have another at any time.'

'No!'

'If he played by the rules, who knows? He could go on for years. But with what sort of quality of life, Holly?'

'So you think he should just lie back and take what's coming?' She was appalled and frightened.

'I'm not saying that at all. Matt's work is his life. Take it away and he might as well be dead as far as he's concerned. Matt believes what he wants to believe. He's made up his mind that he's going to get back to work. Nothing we can say is going to change that.'

She swallowed hard, feeling the tears well up, stinging at her eyes. 'So what do you suggest?'

'We carry on and try to give him some space. He must have weighed up all the arguments, Holly. One way or another, Matt is eventually going to come to terms with it.'

'But. . .wouldn't it be kinder to tell him the truth? Make him see sense?'

'Do you want to be the one to do it?'

'I have to do *something*.'

A nerve pulsed in his jaw as he drew her slowly towards him. 'Sometimes the hardest thing in the world is to do nothing.'

'I'm not sure I can do that.'

'Yes, you can, Holly, because you know it's what he wants.'

She felt the breath catch in her throat as his hands cupped her face, bringing her so close that her nostrils were invaded by the clean, musky smell of him. His sensuous mouth was just a breath away. Shock briefly widened her eyes as he bent his head slowly to brush his lips against her mouth.

She stood, stunned by the power of the sensations that coursed through her. His warm breath fanned her throat as he stared down at her. She felt his gaze sweep over the creamy translucence of her skin and she began to tremble as his head lifted and, for a moment, he looked into her face.

This shouldn't be happening, she told herself. She made a soft sound of protest, trying to turn her head away, but he wouldn't allow it, pulling her closer still, if that was possible, until she couldn't help being aware of the taut maleness of his body.

'What are you so afraid of, Holly?' he rasped. 'You must know I'd never hurt you?'

Not intentionally, maybe, the thought hovered. She

was aware of the sensuous mouth above her own before it descended, brushing aside her denial as she clung to the rapidly fading remnants of her resistance.

The warmth of his body permeated through her clothes, making her all too aware of his arousal, of his vital strength. Then, to her everlasting shame, she stopped struggling as a totally new sensation coursed through her, so breathtakingly exquisite that, almost against her will, she found herself responding.

It was a long time since any man had aroused her to a sense of sexual awareness. Even with Martin it had never been quite like this. Their lovemaking had been gentle, fun. Nothing had prepared her for this almost primordial feeling, or her own body's traitorous response. Sam Stratton was the most sexually exciting man she had ever met.

A tremor ran through her. She felt both shocked and appalled. What was she doing? How could she forget so easily?

'Please, no,' she breathed raggedly, her hand pressed against him as she tried to twist away.

She felt him tense. He stared at her, a nerve pulsing in his jaw, then, abruptly, he let her go.

'You're right. I think it's time I left, before I do something we might both regret,' he rasped. 'Goodnight, Holly, and sweet dreams.' His mouth twisted. 'They're safer than the real thing.'

She stared after him for several seconds, before finally making herself a fresh cup of coffee, stirring in sugar lethargically. It wasn't as if there was any reason why she should let him affect her like this and yet it seemed to happen, that feeling that the moment he walked into view he presented some kind of threat.

But it didn't have to be like that, she chided herself. Furiously she put her cup down and went briskly from room to room, plumping cushions with far more vigour than they warranted, tidying magazines, dusting the furniture until she came to a halt, breathing hard.

This is ridiculous, she told herself, brushing a hand against her eyes. She had her life all neatly mapped out and it didn't include getting involved, especially with a man like Sam Stratton. Getting involved made you vulnerable, and she had no intention of laying herself open to that kind of pain ever again.

Easy to say. What she had failed to take into account was a man like Sam Stratton, but at least now she recognised the dangers and could be on her guard.

CHAPTER FIVE

FUME-BLACKENED snow lay in heaps against the hedges. The roads had cleared but the fields still lay covered by frozen snow, impervious to the efforts of the watery winter sun.

Driving along the lanes, Holly stifled a yawn as she switched on the car radio.

'. . .followed by more snow in the north,' announced the unbiased voice.

Well, if that's the best you can do, I'd rather not know, thank you very much.' Silencing the radio again, she slowed to pass a walking figure ahead. Frowning, she stared into the rear-view mirror, then slowed and came to a halt. Leaning over, she wound down the passenger-side window as the figure drew level.

'Joe? It *is* you—I wasn't sure. I didn't expect to see you out here, not by yourself, anyway. Can I give you a lift somewhere?'

'No, thanks all the same, Doctor.' Joe Blunsden, heavily muffled in coat, scarf and cap, peered in at the window. He coughed wheezily and Holly felt a pang of alarm.

'It's a biting wind out there, Joe. Not a day to be out walking. So where's Moss, then? Curled up in front of the fire? I don't think I ever remember seeing you without him.'

The old man's face crumpled. 'Moss's gone missing. I can't find the daft old beggar anywhere.'

'Oh, Joe.'

'Aye, he were in his kennel last night, same as always, when I went to bed. Come this morning, I went

88

down and 'e was gone.' He shook his head, a hand gripping the open window. "E'll not last for long, not on 'is own, not in this.'

'But he can't have wandered far, Joe.'

He straightened up, staring around him. 'I thought I'd look where we go for our walks. 'E may have took it in 'is 'ead to have a sniff around. But it isn't like 'im.'

'Well, I'm on my way to the surgery, Joe. I'll keep my eyes open, and if I see him I'll try and persuade Moss to come with me, or I'll give you a call. But don't get too cold, now.'

Waving, she went on her way, her eyes scanning the roadside, but to no avail. When finally she arrived at the surgery, it was to find the waiting-room already filling up. Shivering, she closed the door quickly on a flurry of snow as she made her way to the office.

'It's a cold morning out there.' Betty looked up, smiling, as she sorted the morning mail. 'These are for you, Doctor.'

'I know, it's freezing.' Chafing her hands, Holly accepted the pile of letters. 'I passed Joe Blunsden about ten minutes ago. He looked frozen to the marrow.'

'You don't mean he was out walking in this?'

'I know.' Holly frowned. 'I'm worried about him.'

'Worried about whom?' Sam spoke from the doorway. He was carrying his jacket slung over one shoulder, revealing tautly muscled arms and chest beneath a white shirt. His hair was darkened by a few flakes of melting snow. Holly had to resist as almost compulsive urge to run her fingers through it.

'It's Joe Blunsden. I've just passed him a couple of miles or so back on the road. He's out looking for his dog.'

Sam's gaze went to the nearby window. 'Not exactly the day for it, is it?'

'That's what I'm afraid of. He's nearly eighty and not exactly in the best of health.' She bit at her lip. 'I expect Moss will turn up. It's not like him to go wandering off. Those two are usually inseparable. Anyway, thanks, Betty. I'd better make a start.' Waving the bundle of letters, she turned away.

'Holly, wait.' Sam's hand caught at her arm, sending a mass of ill-timed signals flaring through her veins. Her head rose and she felt the full weight of those blue eyes studying her. Warmth flooded her face and it was a relief to hear her voice sounding so normal.

'I'm really busy. I have to make a few phone calls before I start surgery. . .'

'It won't take long. I just thought you'd want to know, I rang the hospital and got a report on Fran Waring.'

'Oh!' Her interest caught, she smiled. 'Is she all right?'

'She's settled rather better than we dared hope.'

'Relief, possibly. I imagine, deep down, she must have known she couldn't carry on. It must have been a dreadful worry for her niece. Still, at least she knows her aunt is being cared for. What about the chest infection?'

'Obviously they put her on antibiotics. It's early days yet, and you know there's always a risk of pneumonia with elderly patients, but, yes, they think she's responding.' Sam smiled. 'That, plus the fact that they're starting to build up her fluid levels and nutritional intake——' he nodded '—makes the picture a lot brighter. Her poor physical state could probably account for her confusion.'

'So, what's the prognosis?'

'I'd say much brighter. She may need a brief spell of recuperation, but I see no reason why, with the proper support, she shouldn't go home in a couple of weeks or so.'

'Oh, that's marvellous. . .'

'Excuse me, Doctor.' A patient came out of the treatment-room, apologising as she edged past them in the narrow corridor. Instinctively Sam drew Holly aside, his arm round her as, smiling, the woman made her way out.

For several seconds she was held within the warm circle of his arm. His skin smelled faintly of aftershave and, once again, she was totally unprepared for the primitive way in which, for those few seconds, she seemed to respond to that brief contact.

She stiffened, half stepping back as her gaze shot upwards into the blue eyes which regarded her with a hint of amusement. Taking several deep breaths, she said briskly, 'Yes, well, if you'll excuse me, I do have some work to do.'

The empty consulting-room was like a tiny oasis of peace in the untidy jumble of her thoughts. Shedding her coat, she checked her appearance in the mirror: fashionable, straight knee-length skirt, vivid, bronze-coloured silk shirt.

Seating herself at the desk, she hitched her skirt into place and pressed the buzzer, summoning her first patient of the day.

Luckily it was a fairly routine morning and she finished early, while Sam was still seeing the remainder of his patients.

'Right, I'm off to try and get through my calls,' she announced at the desk.

Julie handed her a list. 'There aren't too many.'

'Great, that's what I like to hear. I'll do these two first, then I want to call in on Uncle Matt, and I'll make Frank Haskins the last call on my way back. I should be a couple of hours, if all goes well. See you later.'

Parking her car in the drive of her uncle's house, she let herself in by the kitchen door to be greeted by the housekeeper. Mrs Reynolds's face lit up with pleasure.

'Oh, Doctor, how nice to see you. The doctor will be pleased. Now, you go through. I was just making some coffee. I'll pop another cup on the tray and bring it through.' Her glance went disapprovingly towards the open door. 'Perhaps now you're here you'll be able to talk some sense into him, because I certainly can't.' It was teasingly said, but Holly caught an undertone of concern.

'I'll do my best, Annie, but I know even before I start that I'm fighting a losing battle.' She frowned. 'How does he seem?'

'Much as you'd expect for a man who won't listen to good advice.' Annie Reynolds rattled cups on to the tray with untypical vigour. 'I may not be a doctor but I can see when he's doing more than he should. But will he listen?' The older woman's mouth tightened. 'That phone never stops ringing, for a start. If it's not one committee, it's another——'

'Holly, darling. I thought I saw your car. What a lovely surprise.' Matthew Wainwright wandered into the kitchen. 'I was just about to have some coffee. We'll have it in the library, if there's any chance we'll ever get it, that is,' he muttered grumpily.

Annie sniffed disdainfully, putting biscuits on to a plate, and Holly hid a smile.

'You're an old grouch. Annie's a treasure. She only worries about you.'

'Of course she does, and I appreciate it, but I can't abide fuss, you know that. Come on, let's go and sit by the fire.'

'I can't stay long. I'm supposed to be doing my calls.'

'Long enough to have some coffee, though.' He tossed aside a pile of magazines and sank into a chair.

Holly purposely directed her attention from the tinge of grey round his mouth, the lines of tiredness in his face. 'I hope you've not come to lecture me too.' He rummaged for his pipe.

'I wouldn't dream of it.' Although that was what her instincts told her to do. 'I know I'd be wasting my time. But I do worry about you. You know you should be taking things more easily and the pain is troubling you, isn't it?'

His mouth hardened for an instant. 'It's nothing— nothing for you to worry about, anyway. Annie's a good soul but not the best cook in the world. The odd spot of indigestion's not so out of the way at my time of life.' Suddenly his eyes were serious. 'Don't worry about me, Holly, my dear.' He leaned forward, patting her hand. 'I'm happy doing what I do, so let's leave it at that, shall we?'

Helping herself to coffee, Holly reflected unhappily that Sam was right. Sometimes the hardest thing in the world was to do absolutely nothing.

It was still freezing outside as she finally left to make her calls. Consulting her list, she made for one of the outlying farms, abandoning her car at the gate and deciding to walk the rutted narrow lane.

Slipping her feet into her boots, she set off, her breath fanning white into the air, thankful that the track was frost-hardened rather than the more usual muddy quagmire.

The patient turned out to be a fractious four-year-old who was obviously running a temperature.

'I'm sorry to call you out, Doctor,' the anxious mother insisted as she ushered Holly upstairs. 'As a rule, nothing would keep William in bed. He's usually rushing around, getting into all sorts of mischief.'

'Don't worry about it.' Holly smiled. 'When a child is quiet it's usually a pretty sure sign that something is wrong. It's the quiet ones we worry about. So, young William——' she put her briefcase down beside the bed, already making a swift, professional assessment of the flushed child '—I hear you're not feeling too well.' Taking off her coat, she sat beside him, taking one small hand in her own. 'Shall we take a look at you and see if we can make you feel better?'

In fact, it scarcely needed an examination to diagnose a textbook case of chicken-pox, but she made the usual investigations before straightening up. 'Well, I'm afraid it's chicken-pox all right, and he's got quite a nasty dose of it.'

'Oh, well, I've been half expecting it. Several of the kiddies at the local playgroup have gone down with it this past fortnight. I was hoping we'd get away with it. The spots came out so quickly.' Liz Glover's tired face relaxed into a smile. 'I found half a dozen spots last night, but by this morning they were pinging out all over the place.'

Holly smiled. 'That sounds pretty typical. I'm afraid he's probably got a few more to come yet, but, if it's any consolation, it's better he has it now than when he's older. Chicken-pox in adults is much more serious. In a few rare cases it can cause some quite dangerous complications. So, young man——' she patted the small hand '—I don't suppose you're going to be doing much running around for a few days.'

Getting to her feet, she followed Liz Glover down the stairs. 'Just let him take things at his own pace. He'll probably want to sleep. Try and get him to drink plenty of fluids, light meals if he wants them, but he should be right as rain in a few days.'

'Can I make you a cup of tea, Doctor?'

Holly looked ruefully at her watch and sighed. 'I'd love one, but I'd better get on. I've still a couple of calls to make. I'd be grateful if I could use your phone, though. Like an idiot, I left my mobile back at the surgery.'

'Of course, help yourself.'

Holly tapped out the number of the surgery. 'Hello, Julie? Yes, I know. I forgot to bring my mobile. I left it on the desk. Perhaps you can rescue it for me? Any more calls? Oh, thank heavens for that. No, I'm just about to leave Fillditch Farm. I should be back at the surgery in. . .say about an hour. Yes, my appointment with Bob Tanner. No, I should be back in plenty of time. I'll see you later.'

It was well past lunchtime and snowing heavily again by the time she had completed the remainder of her calls. It wasn't until she was driving back along the lanes that she realised she was actually tired, and a niggling tension headache was beginning to make its presence felt.

Her hands tightened their grip on the wheel as the car hit a frozen rut and lurched unsteadily. Drawing a sharp breath, she eased up on the accelerator, forcing herself to concentrate. It was a narrow road, made darker by high hedgerows and overhanging trees. The sun's rays hadn't penetrated during the day, which was making driving more difficult.

She shivered, jiggling the fan-heater. It had been behaving erratically for weeks. Another thing she had been meaning to fix, but somehow there was never a right time, or the energy. Still, at least after her appointment with Bob Tanner there was no afternoon surgery, though she would be on call. The thought of a quiet evening spent in front of the fire and watching television was suddenly enormously pleasing.

Uneasily, she realised it was already getting dark. The wind had picked up in the last half-hour, whipping up the powdery snow, and the windscreen was icing up.

At this rate she wasn't going to be back in time for her appointment.

'Damn!' She gritted her teeth as she fought to keep the car steady on the now more open road. Her stomach rumbled and she thought longingly of a bowl of hot soup. The vision evaporated as she took a bend slowly, but the car's wheels failed to grip on a gathering layer of snow and started to skid wildly out of control.

She struggled desperately with the steering-wheel, saw the overhanging branch of a tree looming, and felt an ominous thud which threw her forward in the seat.

For several seconds she sat with her head lowered, feeling breathless and shaken, her hands braced against the wheel, wondering faintly what had happened.

Straightening, she applied her foot to the accelerator, but nothing happened. Jabbing a hand at the wheel in frustration she cut the engine and managed, stiffly, to climb out.

'Oh, no!' She drew an involuntary gasp of dismay as she moved gingerly to the rear of the car. It had skidded and come to rest at an angle in the ditch. In fact, she realised with a shudder, she had been lucky. The overhanging branch had missed her by inches. Not that that seemed much consolation as she viewed the damage. Somehow she was going to have to move the car or get help, and the likelihood of that, on a lonely stretch of road like this, seemed highly unlikely.

Slamming the door, she opened the boot, hunting for the spade which was almost a standard piece of equipment for doctors working in a rural practice. Right now, using it to steady herself in the mound of accumulated snow, and viewing the angle of the car, she didn't feel any great surge of optimism.

She winced as the spade jarred against solid ground. Blowing on her numbed fingers, she struggled breathlessly to shift the layer of earth wedged around the tyres, but no amount of effort would move it. It was no use. The car was well and truly stuck.

She knelt in the snow, feeling the angry frustration welling up. 'Don't do this to me. Not here, not now.' The sound of her own voice startled her. She sniffed hard, using her teeth to tug off a sodden glove and running the back of her hand against her frozen nose.

Her teeth were chattering with cold and, if she admitted it, a sudden feeling of nervousness too. Resignedly she got to her feet, leaning against the car to stare into the growing darkness around her. Her breath spilled white into the air and she hugged her arms around her in a self-protective embrace to stop the shivering which, she realised, was probably due as much to shock as to the falling temperature.

'Well, it looks like a long walk,' she said aloud. 'Either that, or sit here and freeze to death.' Neither option appealed. She suddenly realised that her head was aching where it had been caught a sideways glancing blow as the car had come to an abrupt halt in the ditch, and she thought longingly of the cottage and a cosy fire burning in the hearth.

Shivering, she climbed carefully back into the car to sit, blowing on to her frozen hands, trying to think rationally. If she sat here on the slight off-chance that someone would come along, she might well freeze. It was an isolated road. On an evening like this the locals would probably have no reason to use it.

With one shaking hand, Holly probed the dull ache in her temple and was surprised to see blood. With the other she fumbled in the glove compartment for a map, spreading it out against the steering-wheel, switching on the interior light to study it.

Sighing, she came to the conclusion that walking towards Radleigh was probably the lesser of two evils. Grimly she refolded the map, stared into the darkness for several seconds, then climbed out of the car again, collected her briefcase, slammed the door and started walking.

Her head ached too much to be able to recall where the nearest house or phone might be, but surely, somewhere, there would be a glimmer of light from a farm or a cottage.

Her confidence faded, however, as she came to a halt, breathing hard, and peered at her watch. She guessed she must have covered about a mile, but, with a sense of shock, she realised it had taken nearly an hour. If only she had remembered to bring her mobile phone.

By now it was completely dark. It had stopped snowing but the wind was blowing eerily across the open fields. She kept her head lowered, clutching her collar against her cheeks, gritting her teeth as she forced herself to keep moving. Perhaps she should have stayed with the car. At least it would have offered some protection.

Her clothes were wet and her hands and feet seemed to belong to someone else by the time she first heard the distant sound of an approaching car. She turned, trying to find its direction, only to feel a pang of disappointment. Nothing, no lights. Perhaps she had imagined it.

She turned back the way she had been walking, willing herself to keep moving, lowering her head against the fine, powdery snow which was blowing towards her. Physically drained, she fought down the lump in her throat. She had heard of people dying in conditions like these, but the possibility had never come quite so close to home before.

Then, suddenly, a car's headlights cut through the darkness, coming from behind her. She heard herself laugh aloud with relief. Someone was coming. Trying to step aside, her foot slipped and she sat heavily in the snow and stayed where she was, momentarily too tired to move.

She was still there when, out of the winter darkness, the headlights slid over her. Weakly she raised a hand against the glare. Brakes were jammed on, a car door slammed.

Vaguely she was aware of a figure striding towards her, but only as a pair of strong hands dragged her bodily to her feet did she find herself staring dizzily into a face which was taut with anger and which she recognised only too well.

Even as her head swam and relief surged through her she noticed, with an irrationality she could only put down to exhaustion, that flakes of snow had settled in his hair and that he was struggling out of his jacket.

'You crazy little fool. What the hell do you think you're doing?'

Holly's teeth rattled. 'I was walking.'

'I can see that.' Sam stared down at her, his eyes dark, and, for some reason she couldn't fathom, angry. 'I found your car about a mile back along the road.'

Her head jerked back with the force of his shaking and a feeling of resentment rose in her, making her suddenly angry. 'The car slid on a patch of ice and went into the ditch. I tried to move it. . .'

'You little idiot.' He was breathing hard. 'Have you any idea what——?'

She tried to push him away. She didn't need this right now. 'It was an accident,' she bit out in retaliation. 'You don't seriously imagine I chose to get stranded.' She fought to free herself but he didn't release her; instead, his grip tightened.

'I suppose you realise you could have been killed.'

'You're exaggerating.' She knew she sounded slightly hysterical but somehow she couldn't help it.

'You're not making sense.' Sam pulled her closer, his gaze searching her pale face. She heard him suck in a breath. 'You're hurt.' His hand reached out to examine the cut on her temple.

'It's a scratch, that's all. I'm perfectly all right.' Apart from a splitting headache and feeling sick. Serves you right for skipping lunch, she thought. 'Anyway, how did you know. . .?'

His mouth was a grim line. 'I just happened to be in Reception when you phoned through earlier. Julie said you were due back this afternoon. When you didn't turn up and the weather got worse. . .'

She glared at him. 'I didn't ask you to come rushing to the rescue.'

'At least you admit you needed rescuing. Maybe I should have left you to it.'

She became conscious of the warm, masculine strength of him as he pulled her closer. 'So why didn't you?'

'That's what I'm asking myself.' His eyes glittered angrily. 'I'm not sure I want to know the answer. Or maybe we should both find out.'

She gasped at the crazy electric current which seemed to run through her as her body was forced into contact with his. Her voice was uneven as she tried to push him away, but his head came closer. She tried to turn away but he held her, forcing her closer still and, even as her lips parted on a protest, his mouth came down on hers in a kiss which was both expert and brutal.

She tried to struggle, but it was useless. The more she fought him the more demanding the kiss became, until the barriers of her resistance seemed to crumble and, with a tiny sob, she clung to him. Her head was spinning and her legs felt ridiculously weak. His mouth was hard against her yielding lips and she gave a soft, involuntary moan of pleasure.

He released her with an abruptness which seemed almost as cruel as the kiss itself had been. She swayed, brushing a hand against her forehead. With a muttered oath he caught her in his arms.

'You're a stubborn creature, Dr Palmer. Come on, let's get you back to civilisation.'

'But. . .my car. I can't just. . . I need it.'

His mouth tightened. 'I've got a tow-rope. I'll pull it out of the ditch. I had a quick look at it. By some miracle, there doesn't seem to be any real damage.' He held her at arm's length. 'Do you feel up to driving it back?'

'Yes.' She nodded, and wished she hadn't as her head resumed its throbbing. 'I'm just cold, that's all, and a little bit shocked, maybe.'

'Come on, then, the sooner we get it shifted the better.'

Half an hour later they drew up outside the cottage. Detaching the tow-rope, Sam helped Holly to climb out. She was surprised to find that she was still shaking as she stared up at him.

'Look, I'm really grateful. I don't know what I would have——'

'Forget it,' he grated.

'I can't. I don't want to.' A sudden thought hit her and she groaned. 'Oh, no.'

He was instantly all concern. 'Holly, what is it?'

'Bob Tanner. He had an appointment.'

'I saw him.' He saw her eyes widen. 'You weren't back. He was waiting. It seemed logical rather than send him away.'

She swallowed hard and nodded. 'I'm sorry.' She knew she should move, but her feet felt as if they were glued to the ground and she had to clamp her teeth together in an effort to stop them chattering, yet it wasn't even as if she was cold any more. It was ridiculous. So were the tears which suddenly welled up in her eyes.

In one swift movement Sam's arms were round her. The contact sent a new rush of desire running through her. It was crazy, but she didn't seem to be able to prevent it. Her face lifted to his. She felt him tense, then he set her free, breathing hard.

'You'd better get out of those wet clothes. You need some food and a long soak in a hot bath.' His voice was curt. She couldn't speak. Her pulse was racing crazily. Sam stared at her and his face darkened as she didn't move. 'For God's sake, don't stand there like that or I may change my mind, and then we'd both be sorry.' He turned away, slamming the door of the car. 'Goodnight, Holly,' he rasped. 'Go to bed. I'll see you in the morning.'

He was right: the long soak in the hot bath had taken the chill out of her bones, she had managed to eat something and had finally fallen into bed, determined on an early night, only to find, frustratingly, that sleep eluded her.

Lying awake, staring up at the ceiling, she found her thoughts drifting restlessly back to the events of the afternoon and her response to Sam's kiss. Emotion suddenly tightened her throat at the growing realisation of the effect he seemed to be having on her nerves.

Defensively she turned, plumping the pillows and burying her head beneath the blankets. It had taken months to create a kind of protective shell around her shattered emotions after Martin had died. She had thought she had succeeded until now.

She sat up, plumping her pillows crossly with her fist, and closed her eyes firmly. But not firmly enough to blot the image of Sam out of her thoughts completely. Blast the man. Why had he come walking into her life, filling it with complications? He had no right at all.

She must finally have drifted off into a heavy sleep about half an hour later, so that, when she woke suddenly to the loud shrilling of the alarm, and gazed disbelievingly at the clock which now said four-thirty, she felt shaky and drugged as she reached out to silence it—except that it wasn't the alarm, it was the telephone.

'Go away,' she groaned into her pillow. 'I'm not on call. You've got the wrong number.'

Not on call. Her sleep-fogged brain latched on to the thought and she sat up shakily, aware of the sudden dryness in her mouth.

'Yes, Dr Palmer speaking.'

Annie Reynolds's high-pitched voice had her pushing away the covers and reaching for her robe. 'Oh, Doctor, I'm so sorry to have to call you. I'm at the hospital. I think you should come quickly. . .'

'Annie, it's all right.' It was almost as if she had a premonition as she heard herself say, 'What's wrong?'

'It's your uncle, he's very poorly.' There was panic in her voice.

'Annie, I'll be right there. I'm on my way.' Raking a hand through her hair, Holly was already heading for the bathroom, dashing cold water on to her face, throwing herself into her clothes. Five minutes later she was running blindly for the car.

'Holly, wait.'

Somehow, Sam was there. Everything seemed to be happening in slow motion. Holly felt as if her breath was stuck in her lungs, needing a desperate effort to drive it upwards. She was vaguely aware of Sam's hand beneath her arm, preventing her from stumbling, as if he sensed that without it she would have fallen.

He was wearing dark trousers and a black sweatshirt and, ridiculously, she noticed that he needed a shave. Lines of strain and tension were etched round his eyes and mouth. 'Holly, what's wrong?'

She heard her own voice sounding strangely calm, and wondered how it was possible when her whole brain was in turmoil.

'It's Uncle Matt.' Her breath came in short, painful gasps as she tried desperately to pull away, intent on unlocking her car door. 'He's at the hospital. I have to get to him *now*.'

CHAPTER SIX

'WE'LL take my car.'

'There's no need. . .'

'Holly, don't argue. There's no way I'm going to leave you. Just get in.'

Sam's softly spoken words brought her back to reality and she found herself moving instinctively, her actions becoming automatic. It was almost a relief to do as she was told. She let her head fall back against the seat, his nearness somehow helping as he drove through the darkness.

'Do you know how bad he is?'

'It's his heart.' She had to moisten her dry lips with her tongue. 'Mrs Reynolds said it was bad. She called the ambulance. . .' Her voice broke. 'Thank God she called the ambulance. She phoned me from the hospital.'

Sam cast a quick glance at her stricken face. 'He's still alive, Holly. Bear up, he's going to need you.'

She nodded, her throat so tight that speech hurt. A thought penetrated her befuddled senses and she looked across at his grim profile. 'How—how did you know?'

He took his eyes briefly from the road. 'I heard your phone ringing. I knew you weren't on call, so when it kept on ringing and you didn't answer I knew it had to be personal and some kind of emergency. Matt was the logical conclusion.'

'I'm grateful.'

They reached the hospital and she climbed, shivering, out of the car. Sam's arm tightened round her. 'Come on, they'll have taken him to the coronary unit. Just hang on.'

He was beside her as they walked the seemingly endless length of the corridors. Doors opened beneath the firm pressure of his hand and he guided her through.

'I want to see him,' she insisted.

But the doors of the unit were closed, quietly excluding her. Doctors came and went, some of them familiar figures, but she scarcely noticed.

'I'll make some enquiries.' Sam led her gently to one of the chairs. 'He's getting the best possible care, Holly. For now it's best you let them do what they have to do.'

She knew he was right. He brought her coffee. It was hot and too strong but she drank it anyway, watching the doors, trembling each time a nurse appeared, only to smile and bustle away.

Annie Reynolds came down the corridor towards them, her face white and tear-stained. 'Oh, Doctor, I'm so glad you got here. I was so frightened. I heard him fall and went into his room. He was just lying there and I didn't know what to do.'

Holly was on her feet, hugging the older woman. Sam left them alone, disappearing in pursuit of one of the doctors.

'You did absolutely the right thing,' Holly said. 'Have they told you anything?'

Annie Reynolds shook her head. 'They whisked him away, said it was best I waited here. That's when I phoned you.'

'I'm so glad you did.' Holly brushed a strand of hair from her eyes. 'I feel I should have known. When I saw him earlier I could sense that something wasn't right.'

'The doctor always was a stubborn man. I knew, some days, he was in pain, but he always insisted it was his indigestion.'

Sam came back. Holly found herself desperately searching his face. 'I've spoken to the staff nurse.'

'How is he?'

His hand tightened over hers. 'He's holding his own. It *was* a heart attack. As yet, they don't know how serious. They've managed to stabilise him.'

'I want to see him.'

He took one look at the obstinate set of her mouth and nodded. 'Just for a minute, and he won't be able to talk.'

Sam led her into a small room where a nurse was checking the monitors. Holly stared at the frail figure in the bed, surrounded by wires and tubes. She had seen it all before so many times, but somehow it was different when it was Uncle Matt lying there with his eyes closed, the oxygen mask over his nose and mouth. Suddenly the pretence was swept away. It wasn't indigestion any more. He looked older and smaller and very vulnerable.

'Come on,' Sam said gently. 'I'm taking you home.'

'I want to stay.'

'There's nothing you can do.' Sam led her, protesting, away. 'The doctors say he's stable and resting. They've done what they can to make him comfortable. What he needs now is to sleep, and time for the medication to work. He'll need you to be strong too, Holly, and you won't be if you're dead on your feet.'

She knew it made sense. 'What about Annie?'

'She's gone home. She followed the ambulance in her own car. I said we'll let her know the instant there's any news.'

Holly nodded, feeling a sudden wave of exhaustion hit her again. She was glad he didn't attempt to make conversation as they drove back. Too many thoughts were spinning round inside her head.

Back at the cottage she climbed wearily out of the

car. It was beginning to get light, and suddenly the day stretched ahead. She shivered, and instantly Sam was all concern.

'You're cold.'

Cold was only part of it: she was cold and tired and confused. Right now she didn't want to think about anything except that Sam was there.

'Will you be all right?' His face was grim as he reached out for her and a sob caught in her throat. 'Holly?'

She stared at him, swallowing hard. 'I should have known. I could see what was happening. . .'

His hands closed over her arms. 'You're tired, you're not thinking rationally.'

'I should have done something. . .anything.'

'Like what? There was nothing you could have done. It was going to happen sooner or later,' he said softly. 'You've got to start thinking positively. At least he's getting the best possible care.' He looked at her, a frown drawing his dark brows together. 'You're exhausted. I don't suppose you got much sleep last night?'

Her lips curved in a wry response. 'Not a lot.'

'So, go back to bed. Take the day off.'

'I can't do that. Surgery starts in. . .' She looked at her watch and gave a gasp of disbelief. 'Oh, my. . .in just over an hour.'

'Don't worry about it. I'll cover. In the circumstances the patients will understand.'

She hesitated. 'I do need to make a few phone calls, to my mother in particular.'

'In Australia.'

She nodded. 'She's Matt's sister, after all. The problem will be to stop her getting the next plane over.'

'There's not much she can do, not at this stage.'

'No,' Holly sighed. 'She and Doug were planning to come over in the spring.'

'Do you have to tell her yet? Wouldn't it keep—for a few days, anyway?'

'Matt's not out of the wood yet.' She frowned. 'The next few hours are going to be critical. If anything happened and I hadn't told her. . .

Even so——' she bit at her lower lip '—I can't let you. . .'

'Why not?' His lips curved in a wolfish grin as he drew her against him. 'In case you hadn't noticed, Dr Palmer, I'm all grown-up now. I can handle it.'

In desperation she tried to draw away, and sensed a tautening of his muscles.

'You don't have to run away from me, Holly.' His voice was very soft. He moved to kiss her, very gently, his lips merely brushing against hers, yet it was enough to make her feel as if her body was on fire. She closed her eyes, then her head went back as she let herself be swept along on a tide of emotions. An involuntary shiver ran through her and she stared at him blindly, aware of an unaccountable sense of loss as he drew away.

'I think I'd better go,' he breathed. 'I'll see you tomorrow.' And he was gone, striding away so that she wondered as she let herself into the cottage, closing the door firmly behind her, whether he had actually kissed her, or had she imagined it?

Two days later it had stopped snowing, the sun was shining, and a layer of frost covered the fields as Holly drove to the surgery, where Betty greeted her arrival with a smile

'We've had a couple of cancellations.' She flipped through the appointments book. 'Mrs Appleton rang to say young Hannah seems to be getting over the throat bug by herself. Her temperature is down, and she doesn't want to bring her in unnecessarily. She'll just keep her off school for a few more days, just to be on the safe side.'

'That's fine.' Holly peered at the bundle of letters on the desk.

'And Mr. . .Richards.' Betty tapped the page. 'He was booked in for the last appointment but can't make it after all. I've shifted him to tomorrow.' She frowned. 'I hope you don't mind, but Julie asked if I could fit her in to see you today?'

'Julie?'

'Yes, she knows you're busy, but I get the impression it's urgent, so I slotted her in at the end, if that's all right?'

'Yes, of course, it's fine.' Holly frowned. 'Did she say what the problem is?'

'No, but I get the feeling that, whatever it is, it's been on her mind for some time.'

'Mmm, I know what you mean. Well, I'll see her later, then. In fact, it's probably best that I see her last. That way I can give her more time.'

'Is there any news of Dr Wainwright?'

'I saw him briefly last night and phoned the hospital first thing. He had a peaceful night and they say he's comfortable.'

'Oh, well, that's good news.'

Holly's mouth curved in a wry response. 'I suppose it is. The trouble is, given the least encouragement, Uncle Matt will be running the ward, or doing the rounds of any of his patients who just happen to be in for treatment.' Her blue eyes clouded briefly. 'It's still early days.'

'Yes, but surely he'll have learned his lesson?'

'I wish I had your confidence.' Smiling, Holly made her way to her consulting-room, sat at her desk, drew a

deep breath and called her first patient. 'Ah, Mr
Barratt. How's the diet going?'

It was a routine morning. An hour and a half later
she was entering her notes on to the computer when
someone tapped at the door. Julie hovered uncertainly
in the open doorway.

'Look, are you sure this is all right? I mean, I should
have made a proper appointment. I can always come
back another——'

Holly was instantly on her feet. 'You did have a
proper appointment and now is fine. Come in and sit
down.' Smiling, she gestured towards the chair. 'Take
your time and tell me what the problem is. I get the
feeling something's been bothering you for a while.'

Julie bit nervously at her lower lip as she stared down
at her hands. 'I know I should have come to see you a
while ago, but. . .well, I've been putting it off.' She
glanced up and Holly noted the pallor in her cheeks. 'I
kept telling myself I was imagining things, that—that I
was mistaken, or it was the wrong time of the month.
I'm probably wasting your time.'

'Well, I hope you are,' Holly offered the smiling
reassurance. 'Tell me what's wrong.'

'It's. . . I—I've got a lump, here.' She rested a hand
against her breast. 'It's not very big.'

'Why don't you just slip off your blouse so that I can
take a look?' Holly was on her feet. 'Right, now
whereabouts?'

She made a gentle but thorough examination. 'Ah,
yes.' She could feel the tiny lump. 'Is it painful?'

'No, that's the thing. I didn't notice it until I was in
the bath, and even then I thought I might be mistaken.'

'You do a regular breast examination?'

Julie pulled a face. 'I know I should, but I forgot, or
didn't think it was that important.' With an effort she

managed to smile. 'This sort of thing happens to someone else, not to me.'

'You'd be surprised how many times I hear that.' Holly completed her examination. 'OK, you can slip your blouse back on.' She returned to sit at the desk. 'Have you noticed any other changes in your breast? Any discharge?'

'No.'

'Well, that's good.' Holly looked at the girl as she sat down. 'I'm as sure as I can be that this is simply a fatty cyst and that you've nothing to worry about. But to be one hundred per cent certain, I'm going to arrange an appointment for you at the hospital. They'll probably want to do a mammogram—you know that that's a simple breast X-ray. I'll also arrange for you to see Max Preston. He'll put your mind at rest.'

'And if it's a cyst?'

'He may aspirate it there and then—that is, draw off the fluid.'

'But what if it isn't. . .just a cyst?'

'Don't imagine the worst. I know it isn't easy but try to think positively. Even in those cases where a lump does turn out to be something more serious, these days, with early detection and treatment, the majority of cases are completely treatable. But look, let's get the appointment arranged, and I know it's easier said than done, but try not to worry.'

The other girl managed a rueful smile. 'I do feel better already for having talked to you. I wish I'd done it sooner.'

'I wish most people in the same situation would see me sooner.' Holly smiled slightly as she saw the girl out. 'Apart from the fact that they could save themselves an awful lot of anguish, if there was a real problem, the sooner we find it the more easy it is to deal with.'

'I'll try to spread the word.' This time Julie grinned as she made her way out. 'Thanks again, I'm really grateful.'

Holly was tidying her desk and checking her briefcase when someone tapped at the door and came in. She frowned, certain that Betty had said there were no more patients. Looking up, she saw Sam.

'Oh, hello.'

'Sorry, am I interrupting?'

'No, of course not. Come in.' Smiling shyly, she said, 'I've just finished. I was trying to get myself organised before I do my calls.' She reached for her briefcase and frowned.

'Is this what you're looking for?' Sam held out the list before turning to study the small water-colour she had hung on the wall. He moved closer, peering at it more closely. 'This is good.'

She stared at his broad back, the wide shoulders and lean hips, her mind strangely unfocused until he straightened up.

'Yes, I like it. It's by a local artist.'

He nodded. 'Is there any news of Matt?'

'I phoned the hospital first thing this morning. Apparently he had a good night and he's comfortable——' She broke off, biting on her lower lip as she snapped the locks on her briefcase. 'Comfortable!' She swallowed hard and her gaze skittered away from his. 'What the hell does that mean?'

His gaze narrowed as he moved closer, his hand coming down over her clenched fingers. 'It means he's fighting back, and that's half the battle. Matt's not a quitter, Holly, but he needs you to be strong, too.'

She knew he was right. Blinking hard, she nodded. 'I know. I'm being silly.'

'It's a perfectly natural reaction,' he said softly, his hands moving to her shoulders, drawing her to face him. 'I'd like to see him myself, if that's all right? Just for a minute or two. How about if I pick you up?'

'You don't have to.'

'I'd like to. Besides, there's no point in taking two cars. I'll see you tonight, then.' He drew her towards him. 'He'll be all right, Holly.' His lips brushed against her mouth. 'Trust me.'

She wanted to, she thought breathlessly as he released her and strode away, but right now she wasn't even sure she could trust herself, certainly not where he was concerned.

The rest of the day seemed to pass in a haze of visits, afternoon surgery, and a dash back to the cottage to take a hasty shower and swallow a quick cup of coffee before dressing in black ski-pants and a bright, chunky sweater, and grabbing her jacket.

She felt exhausted, she realised, as she hurried out to Sam's waiting car, to sit docilely as he tucked a rug over her knees. Suddenly she felt ridiculously glad that he was there.

It was dark by the time they pulled into the hospital car park and made their way along the corridors to the coronary unit. The door swung open beneath the firm pressure of Sam's hand.

Holly walked in, smiling, then came to an abrupt halt, feeling her stomach tighten as she stared at the empty bed where Matt had been just a few hours ago. 'Oh, no!' She was vaguely aware of Sam's hand supporting her as she swayed, then Sister's blue-clad figure came bustling towards them. She was smiling.

'Ah, Dr Palmer and Dr Stratton, isn't it?'

'My uncle, he's not worse?'

'Oh, no, no,' Sister Bridie McCarthy assured her. 'We moved him this afternoon on to the general ward.' Blue eyes twinkled. 'He was getting a wee bit argumentative, so we decided he'd probably be better off if he had a little company.'

Holly closed her eyes as a wave of relief washed over her. 'Thank heavens. When I saw the empty bed. . .'

'I'm sorry about that—we should have warned you, but a bed became vacant so we decided to take advantage. Oh, Nurse——' she waylaid a passing third-year nurse '—Mr Baxter is not to go to the bathroom on his own. Keep an eye on him, will you? Sorry about that.' She smiled ruefully at Holly.

'Can you tell me how he is? I'm sure if I ask him I won't get a direct answer.'

'Ah, well, he's doing as well as you'd expect, for a man who's had a second heart attack. I have a feeling he's a bit too stubborn for his own good, but then maybe that's a good thing. He's been sitting in his chair. He's feeling quite well and he's had a little food.' Her face became momentarily serious. 'I'm sure you know that the next few days will be critical? I know he'll be pleased to see you, but we don't want him to become too tired.'

'We'll only stay for a few minutes.' It was Sam who gave the reassurance.

'Well, in that case. . . Ah, no, there's the phone again. You know where the ward is? Good.' Her attractively slim figure sped away, leaving Holly and Sam to make their way along the corridor to the small, six-bed unit.

When they found him, Matthew Wainwright was lying propped up against his pillows, with his eyes closed. A tray bearing an untouched meal stood on the table. Holly looked at him, her face pale. Sam squeezed her hand and stood aside, allowing her to move closer.

'Hello, Uncle Matt.'

He opened his eyes and blinked. 'Holly, my dear, this is a nice surprise.'

'How are you feeling?'

'I'm fine, a bit tired, but then they tell me that's to be expected.' He smiled, and it was reassuring to see the twinkle in his eyes. 'They never give you a minute's peace in here. There's always someone coming to check this or that, bringing me food I don't want.'

'They're just doing their job,' she chided gently. 'I hear you've been giving Sister a hard time.'

He gave a throaty chuckle. 'I like to keep her on her toes.'

'You're wicked.'

He laughed, then looked at Sam. 'I heard old Fran Waring has been admitted.'

'I'm afraid so.' Sam leaned against the locker. 'She hasn't been looking after herself too well. It was a precautionary measure, but I hear she's doing fine.'

Matt nodded, frowning. One blue-veined hand straightened the sheet. 'She's not had an easy time of it, has Fran, not since her Albert died. She'll not take kindly to being in hospital either. I'd like to know how she is.'

'Uncle Matt, you're not to worry yourself,' Holly reproved him gently.

'I've known Fran too long not to worry. She's not one of life's complainers.'

'Would you like me to pop over to the ward and come back and give you a progress report?' Sam grinned.

'It's kind of you to volunteer, my boy. I'd rest easier, knowing she's not too unhappy. . .but maybe Holly could go.'

'Well, yes, but. . .'

'Good girl.' Matthew Wainwright patted her hand. 'That way Sam and I can have a nice chat and he can tell me how he's settling in.'

Sam's mouth twisted. Holly shot him a look and,

with a sigh, made her way out of the ward. If she hadn't known better, she could almost have sworn Uncle Matt was up to something, but perhaps she was being unfair. It was only natural he should want to feel he was still involved in the practice, if only vicariously.

When she returned to the ward some ten minutes later, Sam was sitting beside the bed and the two men were deep in conversation, unaware of her as she walked towards them, until Sam glanced up, frowning in her direction, and suddenly rose to his feet.

'I'll certainly bear it in mind,' he said evenly to the older man.

Holly told herself she must have imagined the vague air of tension between them as Matthew Wainwright held out his hand. 'It's been good to talk. I can't abide feeling as if I'm being wrapped in cotton wool.' He closed his eyes briefly.

'On the other hand, Sister is a formidable lady,' Sam advised, grinning, as that lady approached, 'and we wouldn't want to get on the wrong side of her, would we?'

'I should hope not, indeed,' Bridie McCarthy said with mock severity as she reached for the thermometer. 'In my experience, doctors make notoriously bad patients.' She smiled at Holly. 'Give them an inch and I've never known one yet who wouldn't take a mile. Time's up, gentlemen, please, and now, Dr Wainwright, here's a nice cup of tea, and I've managed to find you a biscuit or two to help it down.'

'I'll see you tomorrow.' Holly bent to kiss him. 'And just to put your mind at rest, Fran is doing nicely. If she goes on at this rate, she could be home in a couple of weeks.' She grinned. 'Oh, and she said it's not a very good example you're setting and how is it to have a dose of your own medicine for a change?'

Ten minutes later they were in the car and she turned

her head to stare out of the window, almost glad of the darkness as her fear became almost tangible, something to be held off as long as she refused to give name to it. Sam drove in silence for a while, concentrating on the road, then glanced in her direction.

'It's early days yet, Holly, give it time.' His hand closed briefly on her arm, warm and strong.

She nodded, turning to look at his profile, swallowing hard on the tightness in her throat. 'He looked so frail, so. . .old. I can't bear the thought of losing him.'

'Don't, Holly. Don't torture yourself, imagining the worst when it may not happen. He's responding well to the— What the. . .? Oh, my God!' His foot suddenly slammed down on the brake. Holly flung out a hand as he struggled to bring the car to a halt.

'What? What is it?' Shaken, she stared at him.

He cut the ignition and was already flinging open the door, his jaw taut as he climbed out to peer into the darkness. She followed suit, shivering violently as the cold air struck.

'There's something at the side of the road. I almost hit it.'

'I can't see anything.' She peered into the darkness. 'It may have been a fallen branch from a tree.'

'I don't think so. I could have sworn it moved,' Sam said tersely, peering into the thin shaft of light from the car's headlights. 'It was back here.'

'Could it have been a cat or a dog?'

He shook his head. 'It was too big.' She was aware of him stiffening suddenly beside her. 'There.' Head lowered against the fine, driving snow, he was heading towards what looked like a large bundle of rags.

Holly followed blindly, conserving her energy to keep up with him. She watched as he knelt down, then gasped involuntarily, 'Oh, my. . .'

'You know him?' Sam's mouth tightened as he supported the trembling man.

'It's Joe, Joe Blunsden, and. . .Moss.' She dropped down beside him. 'I passed him on the road the other day. He was looking for his dog.'

'Well, I think he's found him.' Sam was a man of speedy reflexes. He grimly pushed aside the man's coat and was feeling for a heartbeat.

'Is he. . .?'

He shook his head. 'He's OK, nearly frozen, but I think he'll be all right. He's lucky—the warmth of the dog probably kept him alive. God knows how long he's been out here.'

'Joe?' Holly chafed one of the ungloved hands. 'It's Holly—Dr Palmer and Dr Stratton, Joe. Can you hear me?'

'Aye.' The muffled response came from behind a scarf. 'What the 'ell are you doing out on a night like this?'

Holly almost laughed aloud in relief. 'I might well ask you the same question. We've just come from the hospital, visiting Uncle Matt.'

'I think it might be a good idea if we turned around and headed straight back there.' Sam gently eased the weight of the dog aside, ignoring its soft-throated rumble of protest. 'I know, lad, but if your master will sit around in the snow. . .'

'I ain't going to no 'ospital.' Joe's voice was suddenly reassuringly strong. 'Just sat down to get my breath, that's all.'

'And fell asleep?' Sam queried gently.

'Aye, well. . .'

'Old Moss here must weigh a fair bit, even though I'd say he probably hasn't eaten for a few days, judging from the look of him.'

'He ain't so bad. Daft beggar wandered off. Gettin'

soft in 'is old age.' Joe's arm was wrapped protectively round the collie as it lay across his knees.

'Yes, well, I think he probably saved your life. Another hour in this temperature and I wouldn't have given much for your chances.'

'Aye,' came the gruff response. 'We've been together a good few years.'

Sam straightened up, taking the animal in his arms as, together, he and Holly helped the old man to his feet. 'I still think you should let us take you to the hospital, just so that they can give you the once-over.'

'Nay, I can't be doing with them places.'

'It's all right, Joe.' Holly smiled. 'We can't force you to go, but at least let us take you and Moss home.' She fondled the collie's ears. 'I think what he needs is a nice warm drink and his bed. The same goes for you.'

'Aye.' Joe sniffed hard, rubbing at his watery eyes. 'Well, that's different.'

Moss lay unprotesting as Sam lifted him gently on to the car's back seat and Holly helped Joe climb in beside him. Fifteen minutes later, Joe was settled before a roaring fire with a mug of tea in his hands and a blanket over his knees as Sam made a gentle examination of the collie. He knelt to stroke the dog's silky fur.

'I don't think he's come to any real harm, Joe. He's probably lost weight but he'll soon make that up. I think he may have a bit of a cough, though.'

'I'll get the veterinary out to give the old fellow a going-over,' Joe said gruffly. 'Damn fool, wandering off like that.'

Sam smiled. 'Maybe he's getting a bit past being given the free run of the countryside. It might be better to keep him closer to home from now on.'

'Don't you worry none, Doctor, he ain't going nowhere from now on, lest I'm with him.'

They finally took their leave and, twenty minutes

later, drew to a halt outside the cottage. Sam switched off the engine and cut the lights. The car was warm and it needed a real effort to climb out. One way or another it had been quite a day, and Holly suddenly felt reluctant to enter the silence of the cottage. The last thing she needed right now was to be alone with her thoughts.

'Well, I suppose. . .' She sighed involuntarily.

Instantly, Sam's gaze narrowed. 'Holly, don't go.'

'It's getting late.'

She heard his soft intake of breath as his hands came down on her shoulders, drawing her gently towards him, and she was shaken by the riot of emotions that coursed through her as, with slow deliberation, he took her in his arms.

'Don't be afraid, Holly.'

Easily said, but he didn't know the dangers. She closed her eyes as his finger gently traced the curve of her cheek, and she felt her breath falter as the sensuous mouth came ever closer, tantalising her with its warm desirability so that her own lips parted on a groan of frustration.

She must have been crazy to think she could remain indifferent. The kiss seemed to plunder her senses, stripping away the frail barriers of resistance she had built around herself. Desire coursed through her. She was appalled by her own weakness where he was concerned. What about her loyalty to Martin? Didn't it count for anything? the voice of her conscience gibed. But she had never felt this way about Martin.

She said hoarsely, 'No, Sam, I. . . Please don't.'

He moaned softly against her hair, releasing her mouth for an instant only to reclaim it again, more brutally this time, as if sensing her reluctance ebbing away.

Don't let it stop, some inner voice pleaded. Don't

ever let it stop. Her hands reached up, her fingers twining hungrily in the softness of his hair.

'I want you, Holly.' His voice was hoarse. 'You must know that.'

She didn't want to fight the sense of urgency which was threatening to engulf her. It had been so long since her body had felt this kind of need, this kind of hunger. Too long since Martin had held her. Would he have wanted her to cut herself off, to live her life with nothing but memories? Was that what she wanted? It would be so easy to let go.

Desire flared out of control as, with that overwhelming acknowledgement of her body's needs, another new sensation joined her reeling emotions.

With a sense of shock she realised that she was within a hair's breadth of falling in love with this man! If she wasn't careful it could happen, if she chose to let it.

A sob caught in her throat and she stiffened in his arms. She tried to drag herself away and felt his arms tighten, saw the look of confusion in his eyes.

'Holly, what is it?'

'No, please, don't.' She closed her eyes, aware of the turmoil in Sam's eyes as she broke free, panicking as she realised how little it would take to make her surrender. If he kissed her again. . .

'I can't. . . I won't be hurt again. I've been through it and I don't intend to let it happen again, not a second time.'

Sam released her abruptly, his face taut as he stared grimly at her. 'You can't run away forever, Holly. Some day it may just happen, and you won't be able to fight it. You have to start trusting someone some time.'

She pressed a shaking hand to her mouth. 'I won't let it.' The words were whispered as he drew away, but she thought in sudden terror that it was already too late. She was already in love with Sam.

CHAPTER SEVEN

DRIVING to the surgery the following morning, Holly found herself dreading the inevitable meeting with Sam. She felt tired and looked it, and a cup of strong coffee and a couple of aspirin at breakfast hadn't helped. She hadn't been sleeping particularly well of late, with the result that she had woken when her alarm rang, feeling out of sorts and even more tired than ever.

She pulled into the car park just as Sam was getting out of his own car. She sat, purposely foraging in her briefcase, hoping he would go in ahead of her, but he turned back to collect some papers he had left on the seat and, as he straightened up, their eyes locked before he slammed the door and strode away. He looked tired too, she thought.

He was standing holding the door open a little impatiently when she finally got out of her car, and she felt his arm brush against her sleeve. It was ridiculous the effect even so small a contact could have on her nervous system, yet his own expression didn't change by as much as the merest flicker of a smile.

It came as a relief in the week that followed not to have time even to think about Sam. An outbreak of measles emptied the schools and filled the surgery. A threatened flu epidemic saw patients asking for vaccinations, so that demand outstripped supplies, and, with the prolonged cold weather, Holly found herself offering advice, mainly to her more elderly patients, on the wisdom of staying warm. Not that the majority needed it. Dales-folk were cheerfully hardened to the elements.

Even so, there were some, the more frail, or those living alone, who gave her cause for concern.

She walked into Reception, smiling as she unfastened her jacket. 'Morning, Julie.'

'Good morning, Doctor, you're nice and early.' She handed Holly the mail and Holly flicked through it, ruefully recognising the inevitable promotions informing her of the very latest in drugs and medical care.

'I'm afraid these are going to have to go to the bottom of the pile. Heaven knows when I'm going to find time to go through them all.' She peered at the list of messages. 'It looks as if it's going to be a busy morning.'

'One of the medical reps asked if you could spare him ten minutes or so.' Julie nodded in the direction of the waiting-room. 'He's been there for about half an hour.'

'How busy is it out there?'

Julie consulted the appointments book. 'Full and overflowing, I'm afraid.'

Holly frowned. 'Well, in that case it might be better if you ask him if he can make it another day. I'd rather see him when I can give him my undivided attention. Unless Dr Stratton can fit him in?'

Julie flipped the page and shook her head. 'He's fully booked too.'

'Well, in that case, I'm afraid he'll have to make it another day. By the way——' Holly paused '—how are you?'

'Oh, bearing up.' Julie gave a slight smile, then groaned as the phone rang. Cupping her hand over the receiver she said, 'I've got my appointment to see the consultant. It's this afternoon.'

'Good. You may have to wait a few days for the results of the mammogram to be read and written up, but let me know how you get on.'

'Will do.' Julie waved. 'Yes, Mrs Duncan. Yes, Friday will be fine.'

Holly shed her coat, checked her appearance in the mirror, sat at her desk and rang the bell for her first patient, who turned out to be two—a fractious four-year-old and a runny-nosed toddler who promptly proceeded to grapple with the contents of a jar of throat spatulas, watched by his weary-faced mother who seemed only too pleased to have the pressure diverted, even temporarily, from herself.

'They've both had coughs and colds for about a week, and they're driving me mad, Doctor. Jason keeps saying his head hurts and Paul is off his food. Well, except for the ice-cream, but he can't live on that, can he?'

Holly retrieved the jar and smiled. 'It won't actually do him any harm, for a while at least, if that's really all he fancies. Let's have a look at you first, shall we, young man?'

It didn't need an examination to tell her that she was seeing a textbook case of measles, but she made the usual thorough investigations, checking the child's throat and feeling for the raised glands.

'It's measles, I'm afraid.'

The woman sighed. 'I had a feeling it might be. Several children in Jason's class at playschool have gone down with it, but I thought I'd better check.'

'You did the right thing,' Holly reassured her. 'They'll both feel pretty grotty until the spots appear, but they'll start to pick up again quite quickly. Don't worry about them not eating if they don't feel like it for a few days, as long as they drink plenty.'

The woman made her way out, ushering the children before her, and Holly smiled and rang the bell for her next patient. The door opened slowly and, looking up from the notes she had just completed, Holly watched with amusement as an elderly figure, muffled in coat, scarf and gloves, edged his way into the consulting-room.

'Do come in, Mr Clarke. How are you today?' A quick glance at the notes reminded her that she had last seen the patient a month ago and that he had a history of chronic bronchitis. He coughed wheezily and Holly felt her heart sink.

'Morning, Doctor.'

'You're still coughing, aren't you?'

Bert Clarke grunted as he sat in the chair. 'Can't seem to get rid of it.'

'No, I'm sure it must be a nusiance.' She glanced at his nicotine-stained fingers and said nothing. At the age of eighty, Bert was not going to change the habits of a lifetime. In any case, the damage was done.

She scanned the notes. 'Let me have a listen to your chest and see if we can find out what's happening in there.'

He sighed a rattling sigh as he rose to his feet and hitched up his shirt. Holly applied the stethoscope, listening carefully, and frowned. 'Right, you can tuck your shirt in again, Mr Clarke.'

Seated at the desk again, she said, 'Well, it still sounds decidedly mucky in there.' Studying the notes on the computer, she frowned. 'When did you actually finish the course of antibiotics I gave you a month ago?'

Bert sucked wheezily at his teeth. 'Can't remember too clear. Not much for taking pills. I swallowed 'em for near on a week.'

'You did finish the course, Mr Clarke?'

'Well, didn't seem no point, not when I were feeling better.'

Holly stifled a sigh. 'Mr Clarke, the important thing about antibiotics is that you must take all the tablets, even though you may start to feel better, otherwise what can sometimes happen is that the infection doesn't clear properly and sometimes it comes back, only worse, a second time.'

She typed out a new prescription. 'I'm going to give you a repeat prescription, but this time you must finish the course. There we are.' She tore it off and handed it to him. 'I'd like you to come back and see me in two weeks' time. You can make an appointment at the desk as you go out.'

Bert Clarke got to his feet, thrust the paper carelessly into his pocket and trundled out, muttering under his breath. She could hear him coughing as he made his way through Reception.

When the last patient had finally left, Holly made her way to the office to find Betty making coffee.

'I thought you might need a cup before you go out.'

'Mmm, you're a life-saver. It's been a pretty hectic morning.'

'Any news of Dr Wainwright?'

Sipping at the coffee, Holly looked at her watch. 'Actually, I'm due to phone the hospital now. By the way, I don't suppose you have last month's copy of the medical journal tucked away anywhere? There was some information on a conference I was particularly interested in.' She hunted, frowning, through a pile of journals. 'I thought I'd send for some details while there's still time.'

'I think Dr Stratton has the copy you're looking for. He asked for it a couple of days ago.' Betty looked at the appointments book. 'He's finished surgery, but I don't think he's gone out on his calls yet. You might just catch him.'

'Damn!' Holly muttered under her breath. Draining her cup, she put it down. 'I'll see if he's still there. See you later.'

She walked along the corridor, coming to a halt

outside Sam's door. Her heart thudded as her hand rose to knock. Did she really want the journal so badly? Yes, she did, damn it. She had been interested in this particular conference for some time and the closing date for applications to attend was looming. Her hand hung, poised in mid-air. This was ridiculous. Sooner or later she had to face him.

She tapped lightly on the door and, for a moment, a feeling of relief swept through her as no one answered. He was out. The evil hour could be postponed. She had already turned away when the door opened and he was standing there, a look of surprise on his face, while she stood rooted to the spot.

He frowned. 'Did you want to see me?'

She swallowed hard. 'No, that is. . . Well, yes.'

He didn't move. 'I have some calls to make. Is it urgent?'

'No, or at least. . .' She summoned a smile. 'I understand you have a copy of last month's journal, but it can wait.'

He paused, then stepped back into the room. 'You'd better come in. It's here somewhere.' Frowning, he moved a pile of papers on his desk. 'Ah, yes, here it is.' He looked at her, his expression unreadable as he handed it over, and for some reason she felt cheated. How could he behave as if nothing had happened? But then, she told herself, nothing had.

'Yes, well, thanks. I'll let you have it back as soon as I've finished with it.'

'How's Matt?'

She turned to the taut face watching her. 'I thought he seemed a little quiet when I saw him yesterday. I'm just about to phone the hospital. I'm off this afternoon. I thought I'd go to see him.'

'I'm sure he'll be pleased.' Sam's eyes were dark and unsmiling as he turned, frowning impatiently as he snapped the locks on his briefcase. 'Anyway, I'd better make a start on these calls. Give Matt my regards.'

'Yes, of course.'

It was like talking to a stranger, except that the face was the same, perhaps a little more weary. 'You have to start trusting someone some time,' he had said, and suddenly she found herself battling against an urge to rush into his arms.

'Sam, please, can we talk?' She half turned to follow him, almost colliding with Julie, who was hovering apologetically in the corridor.

'I'm sorry to interrupt, but there's a phone call for you, Dr Stratton.'

He looked at his watch, his dark brows drawing together. 'Damn! I'm just on my way out. Can you take a message?'

'I think it's a personal call, Doctor, from London. A Miss Crawford? She did say it was urgent that she speak to you.'

'Lisa?' He frowned. 'I'll take it in my office.' Glancing at Holly, he said, 'I'm sorry, was it something important? Perhaps we can catch up with each other later?'

'No.' With an effort she managed to smile and felt her heart contract with misery as she watched him stride away. 'It wasn't important at all.'

Back in her own room, she dropped the journal on to a chair, picked up the phone and dialled the number of the hospital. After a short delay a voice answered.

'Oh, yes, hello, Sister. Dr Palmer here. I was wondering. . . Oh? Yes, I. . .' She tasted the sudden dryness in her throat. 'In what way, cause for concern? Yes, I see. Well, yes, he did seem a little quiet. No, he didn't say.' Holly frowned. 'I think you're right.' She glanced at her watch. 'I have a couple of calls to make, but I'll be there as soon as possible. No, I'm grateful, Sister. Goodbye.'

Replacing the receiver, she was surprised to discover that her hand was shaking. Gathering up her jacket and briefcase, she went through to Reception, depositing the bundle of cards on the desk. 'I'll be off, then, Betty.'

'We'll see you tomorrow, then, Doctor.' Betty glanced up, her smile fading slightly. 'Is anything wrong, Doctor?'

'I'm not sure.' Holly frowned. 'I just spoke to Sister at the hospital. She seems a little concerned about Uncle Matt. Nothing specific but. . . I thought I'd pop over there as soon as I've finished my calls. Anyway——' with an effort she summoned a smile '—I'll see you tomorrow.'

Two hours later she was hurrying along the hospital corridor.

'Ah, Dr Palmer.' Smiling, Sister came towards her.

'I gather you're a little concerned about my uncle.'

Sister indicated the small office. 'Perhaps you'd like to come in. Do sit down.'

Holly sat, though not happily. 'You said you couldn't pinpoint anything specific?'

'That's right.' Sister McCarthy studied the notes she picked up from the desk. 'He's responding well to the medication. He's still not eating a great deal but we're not too worried about that at this stage.' She flipped the page and looked at Holly. 'To all intents and purposes, he's making a steady recovery from the heart attack, but there's something. . . I'm sorry I can't be of more help. I spoke to him earlier this morning and he seemed cheerful enough, but I wonder if something is worrying him? It may be nothing, but obviously if there is something, it won't help his recovery.'

'I'll go and see him and have a chat—see if I can get to the bottom of it.' Holly was already on her feet. 'I'm grateful to you for letting me know Sister. It's possible he's worrying about not being able to help at the practice, in which case I can put his mind at rest.'

Walking on to the bright, airy ward, Holly was able to study her uncle before he became aware of her and she experienced a tiny pang of alarm. He was sitting in a chair beside the bed. A newspaper lay, open but ignored, across his knees. His head rested back, his eyes were closed. She thought he was asleep, but as she moved quietly towards him, his eyes opened and he smiled.

'Holly, my dear, what a lovely surprise.'

'Hello, Uncle Matt.' She bent to kiss him.

'I didn't hear you come in.'

'I'm not surprised, you were miles away.' Smiling, she deposited some magazines and a bag of grapes on the bedside locker. 'Anyway, how are you feeling?'

'I'm fine.' He patted her cheek and waved her to a chair. 'I wasn't expecting visitors. This is a nice surprise. The day seems a bit long sometimes. I'm not used to all this inactivity.'

She felt her throat tighten. 'Oh, Uncle Matt, I know how difficult it must be for you, but you're not to worry. Everything's fine at the practice. We miss you, of course, but. . .'

His hand came out to grasp hers. 'My dear, I've never had a moment's doubt that you'd be able to manage beautifully, and, to be perfectly honest——' his eyes twinkled '—I have to say I haven't missed it too much at all.'

'Well, that's good to hear.' She made a pretence of tidying his locker. 'But you are really feeling. . .?'

'They tell me I'm making excellent progress,' he smiled. 'It's a well-worn phrase. I've even been guilty of using it myself in the past. I'm not entirely sure what it means.' For a fleeting moment the smile faded. 'They keep giving me pills to swallow, taking my temperature, checking my pulse.'

Holly smiled. 'They're doing their job.'

'I hate fuss.'

'I know, but it's for your own good. Don't be so stubborn. Let them help you—that way you'll get out of here so much quicker.' She leaned forward to pour him a drink from the jug, painfully conscious that he seemed thinner. 'Enjoy the rest while you can,' she urged, smiling. 'Believe me, you're well out of it right now, what with measles and the odd dose of chicken-pox, not to mention the flu. Give it a few weeks and you'll be raring to go.'

'It's a nice thought, darling,' he smiled. 'But if there's one thing I've had while I've been in here, it's time. This past week or so has given me a chance to do some serious thinking, to take a good look at my life and to come to a few decisions.'

With an effort, Holly managed to smile. 'I thought the idea was that you had a rest, not——'

'I haven't made any sudden decisions. I've actually been thinking seriously about the future for quite some time. I suppose you could say recent events have helped to clarify things in my mind.' He watched her brush a strand of hair from her eyes. 'Holly, darling, I think it's right you should know, I've asked Sam to stay on.'

She stared at him, still smiling even as her heart gave an odd little lurch. 'You mean you're asking him to stay on as locum for a while longer? Well, yes, that makes sense.'

Matthew Wainwright gave a slight smile as he reached for her hand and shook his head. 'I'm sorry, darling, but that's not quite it. I mean I've asked Sam to join the practice, as a full partner. I know——' he anticipated her response '—I should have discussed it with you, but I came to a decision and I wanted it settled, for my own peace of mind. The thing is, I've decided to retire.'

Holly stared at him. 'You're not serious? But why? Uncle Matt, you'll get over this. . .'

He gave a slight laugh. 'I was never more serious in my life. The truth is, my dear, I like the idea. I've had time to think about it before but kept talking myself out of it for all the wrong reasons. I see that now. Well, now I've had this second warning. I've been lucky.' He held her hand. 'I didn't—don't—want to let you down.'

'There was never any question of that—you must know that?'

'I do know, but it's how I would have felt. Now. . .' He looked at her. 'Sam's a good doctor, and the patients have taken to him. He's good for the practice. If I'm going to hand over to anyone I couldn't find anyone better than Sam.'

She stared at him, feeling the sudden dryness in her throat. 'You mean. . .he would take over as senior partner?'

'He has the experience, my dear. Financially he can do things for the practice that I never could.'

'I see.' She drew a deep breath. 'And what does Sam say about all of this?'

'He's thinking about it.'

Thinking about it. He had doubts, then? Somehow, the thought sat uncomfortably with her as she drove back home. The cottage didn't seem to offer the usual comfort when she returned to it, probably because the fire had gone out and the debris from several cups of coffee still littered the kitchen.

Sighing, she abandoned her jacket, put a match to the fire, flipped the switch on the kettle and hurried upstairs to change into a comfortable pair of jeans and a sweater. Her reflection stared back at her, ridiculously childlike, but there was nothing she could do about that, she decided as she made her way to the kitchen to make coffee and reheat a casserole she had prepared the night before, only to find that her appetite had completely vanished.

Her thoughts were in turmoil as she struggled to imagine the practice without Uncle Matt. He had been there for as long as she could remember, a stable anchor in her life. Of course she had known, deep down, that it would have to happen some day, but to be presented with what amounted to a *fait accompli* and to discover that Sam had known all about it and said nothing. . . And then she was struggling to imagine the practice, and her life, without Sam as part of it.

She removed the hot casserole dish from the oven, wincing as she juggled it on to the top of the cooker, burning her hand in the process, and was sucking her finger when the doorbell rang.

'Damn!' She hurried to answer it and then, as if her thoughts had somehow managed to conjure him up, Sam stood there.

He was wearing jeans and a dark blue sweatshirt that seemed to emphasise the colour of his eyes. He was holding Thomas in his arms.

'I think this belongs to you.'

'Damn!' she said again, blowing on her throbbing fingers. 'You'd better come in. I was just taking something out of the oven.'

'That's a nasty burn.' Sam frowned, following her as she sped back to the kitchen to switch off the boiling pot of coffee she had put on to brew. 'You'd better let me take a look. Burns can be nasty things.'

'I am a doctor, in case you've forgotten,' she snapped belligerently, a riot of conflicting emotions vying for place as, ignoring her protest, he took her hand in his.

He studied the reddening weal and frowned. 'That's nasty. It must be pretty painful. Here——' he turned on the cold-water tap '—hold it under here until the burning stops.'

He held her hand as if she were a child, but there was nothing in the least childlike in the way her body was responding to his nearness.

That was the trouble; her head was telling her one thing but her heart wasn't listening. Her normal common sense seemed to fly out of the window whenever Sam was around, but if it was hard enough now to resist him and stick to her principles, how much more difficult was it going to be if he was to become a permanent fixture in her life? The idea didn't bear thinking of. Tears suddenly welled up. Weakly she closed her eyes and drew a shuddering breath as his sweatshirt brushed softly against her skin, sending more dangerous signals to her brain. She felt him tense.

'Holly, what is it?' His voice was uneven as he drew her towards him. His mouth became suddenly taut. 'It's not Matt? He's not. . .?'

She licked her dry lips. 'He's fine, but no thanks to you.'

'To me?' His dark brows drew together. 'What are you talking abvout?'

She shot him a look. 'Oh, please, don't play the innocent.' Suddenly, anger seemed the best, the only defence she had against him. 'Why didn't you tell me? You must have known it was only a matter of time before I had to find out anyway.'

His gaze narrowed. 'I take it Matt has talked to you?'

She gave a hollow laugh. 'That's certainly more than you've done. When had you planned to get around to it? When it was all cut and dried. Don't I get to have a say in what happens?'

'You're not thinking rationally, Holly.' His eyes were dark as he looked at her.

'I'm not feeling very rational right now,' she flung at him, turning away only to have him take hold of her arm, forcing her to look at him. 'Let go of me,' she gritted.

'Not until you've listened,' he said, in a hard voice. 'You want an explanation—you're entitled to it.' He forestalled her challenge. 'I just didn't feel it should come from me. I hadn't realised you felt quite so strongly about the prospect of having me as a permanent member of the practice.'

'It has nothing to do with that.' Her voice was rough-edged as she faced him. How could she tell him the truth: that to have to see him every day, to work with him, would be to undermine every resolution she had struggled so hard to make? 'It's—it's the way it's been done. I should have been told.'

'I agree——' Sam's voice was suddenly gentle '—in normal circumstances. But these aren't normal circumstances, Holly. This whole thing has obviously been bothering Matt. He's been lying there in that hospital, supposedly getting better, and instead he's been worrying himself sick about what's going to happen to the practice.'

'But nothing will happen. . .'

'He's thinking about you. He's got time on his hands——' his face broke into a smile '—and you know what they say about the devil and idle hands.'

'This isn't funny, Sam.'

'No, you're right.' He relaxed his grip to look at her with narrowed eyes. 'It's not funny and I'm not trying to make light of it. But it wasn't my decision and, while we're about it, let's get to the real nitty-gritty, shall we?

What is it that you're really so angry about, Holly? What are you afraid of? Is it the fact that Matt has asked me to stay? Or that I might decide to take him up on his offer?'

CHAPTER EIGHT

HOLLY stared at him and drew a deep breath. 'Don't be ridiculous.'

'Why is it ridiculous? You've made it pretty clear from the outset that you don't want me here.'

'That's not true.'

'No?' His mouth twisted. 'Well, that didn't sound to me much like an invitation to stay. You could have asked nicely.'

Incredibly, she found her defences crumbling. She even managed to smile. 'You're crazy—I suppose you know that?'

'They say it helps.' His mouth relaxed suddenly. 'The really ridiculous thing is that we're both on the same side. We both want what's best for Matt. We just don't seem to be able to meet in the middle, do we, Holly?'

She couldn't bring herself to look at him. 'Are you saying you've actually made a decision?'

He stood watching as she tidied the work-surface without really thinking what she was doing. As always, his nearness was making her uneasy, then suddenly his hand came down over hers, forcing her to face him.

'I don't want to stay where I'm not welcome. It wouldn't work—not for Matt, not for us. You know how I feel about you. I want you, Holly. I can't change the way I feel.' He drew a ragged breath as he cupped her face in his hands, drawing her urgently towards him. 'My God, do you have any idea of the effect you have on me?'

She moaned softly as his mouth came down on hers, making teasing advances against her cheek, to the hollow of her throat and back to her lips, and before she knew it she was caught within the circle of his arms.

'Sam, this is crazy,' she protested weakly.

'Ask me to stay, Holly,' he murmured, before his mouth took possession of hers.

'This isn't fair.' Her body quivered beneath the onslaught. She moaned as his hands slid beneath her sweater, discovering the exquisite fullness of her breasts. It was utterly crazy, she told herself. Things were moving too fast, out of control.

Eyes closed, she tilted her head back, trying to give herself time to think.

'Tell me you want me to stay, Holly,' he breathed again, before his lips traced the curve of her cheek and shifted to the sensitive lobe of her ear.

She heard her own soft gasp of shock as the contact renewed all the fire of their previous encounters. 'I—I can't,' she groaned softly.

'Don't fight it. Go with it,' he said huskily. 'There's nothing to be afraid of.'

She wanted to believe it. 'Things like this don't happen. . .'

'They do if you let them. You've got to want it.'

'But it's not that simple.'

'It can be.' His shuddery breath whispered against the flushed perfection of her skin. 'All you have to do is let go of the past, Holly.'

He made it sound so easy, and maybe it was. Such a small step to take.

He bent his head again to kiss her, and she was incapable of thinking of anything except the warm pressure of his mouth against hers. She responded unashamedly and was drawn closer against the strong, hard masculinity of him.

'Holly,' he groaned, feathering kisses against her eyes and cheek before claiming her mouth again. 'Don't fight it, don't think, don't try to understand. Just let it happen.'

It was crazy, but she would think about that later, much later. Right now, all she could think of was that it seemed right, that she was where she wanted to be. Her head went back, her hands reached up to tangle in the silky darkness of his hair. . .

It was the sound of the phone ringing that brought her back to reality. Sam cursed under his breath as, instinctively, she tried to move.

'Let it ring.' His lips drew her back, but with the strident ringing common sense returned rapidly, and she pushed him gently away, trying to steady her breathing.

'I can't. It might be a patient.' She heard him swear softly as she reached behind her for the phone, fumbling for the receiver as Sam's face followed her own until she tilted her head away out of reach, and said breathlessly, 'Dr Palmer. Yes. No, of course you're not disturbing me.'

Sam nibbled wickedly at her ear. 'Tell him I'm taking care of that, thank you very much.'

In desperation she pushed him away as the voice said, 'Hello, Holly? Is that you? I'm sorry to call you at home. I wasn't sure what to do, only I'm worried about young Simon.'

She sat up, the laughter slipping from her eyes. 'Helen? Hello. . .no, it's fine. You did absolutely the right thing. Yes, of course I'll come.'

She was aware of Sam straightening up, his face suddenly expressionless. She wanted to draw him back, regain the moment. Her eyes followed him to the door, silently pleading with him to wait.

'I'm really sorry,' the woman's voice repeated anxiously in her ear.

'Helen, don't be. That's what I'm here for. I'll be

with you in about. . .fifteen minutes.' What she wanted to say was, I need my own time right now. But she dropped the receiver back into place and turned to see Sam standing at the door, his face suddenly like that of a stranger again. The kiss might never have been, except that her lips still felt swollen from the pressure of his mouth.

'Saved by the bell,' he said evenly. 'I'd better go. Obviously you're needed elsewhere.'

'Sam.' Her voice dragged out his name, but she knew it would be pointless to go after him. 'Helen is a patient, you know I have no choice.'

'It's all right, I understand.'

But his voice sounded so cool that she almost flinched, and as the door closed behind him she was shocked to find her eyes filling with tears.

'Damn!' She swore under her breath. 'Damn! Damn! Damn!'

The door was open and Helen Watts was waiting for her as Holly manoeuvred her car along the lane leading to the farm and parked in the yard.

She was in her mid-thirties, dark-haired and attractive, and her face was pale and anxious as she waited for Holly to reach for her briefcase before slamming the car door.

'I'm so sorry to have to call you out, only I really didn't know what to do for the best.'

Holly followed her into the warmth of the old farmhouse. 'Don't be—after all, what are friends for?'

Helen Watts gave a grateful smile. 'Trouble is,' she said ruefully, 'I only ever seem to call when there's trouble.'

'It's all part of the job. Anyway, I know you don't call without good reason. You say it's young Simon?'

'That's right. He's through here. We thought it best to let him stay on the sofa in front of the fire where we

could keep an eye on him.' She led the way into the
chintz-furnished room where a young man rose to his
feet, a look of relief on his face as Holly walked into
the room.

'John, how are you?'

'I'm fine.' He gave a slight grin. 'It's this young chap
who's the problem.'

'Hello, Simon.' Holly bent to ruffle the hair of the
flushed seven-year-old who was lying on the sofa. His
eyes were closed and his knees were drawn up beneath
the blanket. Brushing a hand gently against his forehead, Holly could feel that he had a temperature. 'I
hear you're not feeling too well. Can you tell me what's
wrong? Have you got a pain? Can you show me where
it is?'

A small hand came out from beneath the blanket and
settled in the area of his lower abdomen.

'It started this morning. He said he had a tummy-
ache. We thought maybe he'd eaten too much fruit—
you know what kids are. If it's there, they'll eat it. Only
he seemed to get worse.'

The couple watched anxiously as Holly made a gentle
but thorough examination before finally straightening
up.

'Did the pain start in a particular place?'

'Well, yes, sort of to the right, but it moved.'

Holly nodded, watching every fleeting change of
expression on the child's face. 'And where is it now?
Here? Yes, that's all right. I've finished now, Simon.'
She gave the swift, smiling assurance and tucked the
blanket round the small figure again. 'Has he been
sick?'

'Yes, twice.'

Holly nodded. 'And I can see he has a temperature.'

'What do you thing is wrong with him?'

'Well, I can tell you it's nothing desperately serious.'

She lowered her voice as they moved away from the sofa. 'On the other hand, I'm afraid I'm going to have to call an ambulance and get him admitted to hospital. It's appendicitis. He's in quite a lot of pain and it's not going to get any better, so the sooner we get him admitted the better.'

'I had a feeling that's what you were going to say.' Even so, John Watts looked slightly shell-shocked. 'I had it myself when I was a kid. Mind you, I was nearly fourteen.'

Holly smiled as she reached for her mobile phone. 'Yes, well, you'll probably still remember what it was like, and that the only thing you wanted was for someone to make the pain go away. So I'll ring through for an ambulance now.'

'I suppose I'd better get a few things together in an overnight bag?' In spite of her obvious relief, Helen was slightly tearful. 'Will they operate tonight?'

'I imagine so.' Holly put an arm round the young woman's shoulders. 'I know,' she said softly. 'He's still only a baby, but I promise you, he's going to be feeling a lot better once they get rid of what's causing the pain.'

'I know, I'm being silly. It's just that he's never been away from home without me before.'

'Look, if you want to, I'm sure I could arrange for you to stay overnight at the hospital, so you can be with him until he goes to Theatre and see him again afterwards.'

'Could you really?'

'I'll have a jolly good try.' Holly smiled. 'The hospital has a couple of small side-rooms they keep empty especially for parents who need to stay. I'll need to check that they haven't had any serious emergency admissions, in which case those parents would obviously be given preference, but I'll see what I can do.'

Half an hour later, having seen the ambulance bear her patient away, she was on her way back to the cottage. It was late, she felt physically tired, emotionally exhausted, yet, frustratingly, she knew that even if she went to bed she wouldn't sleep. Mentally her brain was in turmoil.

Bringing the car to a halt, she switched off the engine but made no attempt to move, staring out into the darkness instead. The lights were still on in Sam's cottage. Her hands clenched against the wheel.

Suddenly she knew she couldn't leave things as they were. Too much had been left unfinished, unsaid. The more she tried to face the possibility of Sam going away, the more she knew that she didn't want it to happen.

She had kept her emotions in cold storage for so long, imagining they were safe. What she hadn't bargained on was someone like Sam Stratton coming along and rekindling the fires, and the trouble with fire was that you could get more than your fingers burned. But then she wasn't a child any more, she was an adult, and she could see the dangers. For the first time in a long time, she felt she was doing something with her eyes wide open.

Taking a deep breath, she reached for her jacket and briefcase and got out of the car. Standing outside Sam's cottage, she raised her hand, hesitated for a second, then knocked. The door opened, letting out a flood of light. She blinked, then Sam was standing there, solid and real and very, very desirable. He didn't invite her in.

She swallowed hard and, with an effort, managed a smile.

'I'm sorry, I know it's late but I've been thinking. . .

Why don't you come to my place for a meal tomorrow evening? I'm not the world's best cook, but I could manage to cremate a couple of steaks and rustle up a salad. We could open a bottle of wine and. . .' She looked at him, moistening her dry lips with her tongue. He wasn't making this easy. 'I thought. . .maybe we could talk.'

'It's a nice idea.' His voice sounded rough-edged with tension. 'But I'm afraid I can't.'

'I see,' she said flatly, feeling the colour darken her cheeks as she looked at him and, with an effort, managed to force a smile. 'Well, never mind. Some other time, maybe?' She had half turned away when his voice stopped her.

'Holly, I don't play games and I'm not looking for a fight. I was telling you the truth. I won't be here, it's as simple as that. I need to go away for a couple of days.'

She was conscious of a sudden feeling of tightness in her throat. 'I see.' Her chin rose. 'I take it it's important?'

A spasm flickered briefly across his features. 'It's something I have to sort out.'

She shot him a look. 'And it can't wait?'

'I'm afraid not. I have to go to London,' he said evenly. 'Something has cropped up. There are a few things I have to sort out with Lisa.'

Lisa. The call from London. Holly's throat tightened painfully. Of course, she hadn't made the connection until now. Suddenly it all made sense. Shock seemed to hold her rooted to the spot, even though her every instinct was to turn and run. Lisa, the girl from the past. . .except that it seemed she was suddenly very much a part of the present. Holly was shocked to discover that she could actually feel jealous of a girl she had never even met. How could she have been so naïve?

Sam's gaze narrowed. 'I realise it's going to cause some inconvenience.'

'Well, yes, since you mention it, it is rather.' She heard the note of irritation in her own voice but was powerless to stop it.

'I'm only asking you to cover for me tomorrow, Holly. Thursday is my day off anyway.'

'I don't need to be reminded of the duty rota, thank you very much. I'm well aware of when I'm on call.' She took a deep breath and even managed a smile. 'Since it's so important, of course you must go. I suppose I can manage. I'll have to, won't I?'

'I'm grateful.' He looked tired. Lines of strain and tension were etched round his eyes and mouth.

'It's no problem. I'll say goodnight, then.' Without waiting to hear his reply, she turned and hurried away. Don't be grateful, Sam, she thought, as she let herself into her own cottage and firmly closed the door. I don't need your gratitude. Just make sure you come back.

It was raining when she drove to the practice next morning. She had slept badly and, consequently, when she finally had drifted off, had slept so heavily that she had failed to hear the alarm. Her head ached and the sight of a full waiting-room did nothing to improve her temper.

Pausing at the desk just long enough to pick up the morning's list and patients' cards, she flicked through the post and frowned. 'Damn! I was expecting the results of that blood-test I did on Mrs Anderson a few days ago.'

'It may come in the second post.' Betty looked over Holly's shoulder. 'Was it urgent?'

'Yes, it was. Why the hell can't these people get their act together?'

'Would you like me to phone through for the results?'

'Yes. . .No.' Holly ran a hand through her hair, missing the look that passed between the two women. 'When is Mrs Anderson due to come in and see me again?'

Julie flipped through the pages of the diary. 'Not until Friday.'

'Oh, well, I suppose it can wait another day, but if it's not here tomorrow, we'd better start chasing.'

'Will do.' Betty's smile became a look of concern as she followed Holly along the corridor. 'Do you feel all right? You're looking a bit peaky this morning.'

'No, as a matter of fact I've got a splitting headache.'

'Would you like me to make you a cup of coffee before you start?'

'You're a life-saver.' Holly gave a slight grin of apology. 'I don't suppose you could throw in a couple of aspirins as well?'

'Coming up.'

Why was it, Holly wondered as she rang the bell an hour later, that when she was having a bad day anyway, things that would normally have been straightforward turned into something resembling a nightmare?

Harry Bickerstaff was an overweight, ruddy-complexioned seventy-year-old who knew his rights and wasn't about to be denied them. He leaned forward, his finger rapping the desk.

'I had an appointment with that there new doctor.'

'Yes, Mr Bickerstaff. Unfortunately, Dr Stratton was called away. . .'

'We didn't get none of this when your uncle was around.'

'No, I realise it's very upsetting for you, but I'm afraid, on this occasion, it was unavoidable. Dr Stratton will be back in a couple of days. In the meantime, perhaps I can help?'

'It's this.' Harry fumbled in his pocket, producing a

bottle of pills which he dropped on to the desk in front
of her. 'Useless they are, useless. Been taking them for
a week now, and they haven't done a thing for me
backache. What's the good of that, then?'

Holly studied her notes, trying to hide her confusion.
'Mr Bickerstaff, I don't quite understand. . .'

'Simple enough, ain't it?' He wheezed noisily. 'Supposed to get rid of the pain. Well, it ain't working.'

Holly turned from her written notes to the computer,
bringing up the patient's medical history. 'But, Mr
Bickerstaff, according to these notes, I last saw you
eighteen months ago. At that time you complained of a
sore throat.'

'Right.' His chin jutted aggressively. 'You saying
your medicine ain't no good, then? Cheap stuff, is it?
Spot of the sugar sweeties in a fancy bottle? Well, I
ain't nobody's fool.'

Holly's lips quivered. 'Mr Bickerstaff, I promise you,
that medicine is perfectly sound and it does the job it's
supposed to, if it's taken properly.'

Bushy eyebrows rose. 'You saying I can't read or
something?'

'Not at all.'

He reached for the bottle and tapped the label. 'Take
one tablet three times a day, after meals.'

'Yes, that's right.'

'Well, that's what I been doing.'

'Yes, Mr Bickerstaff, but these tablets were prescribed two years ago, for a sinus infection, for your
wife.'

'Painkillers, ain't they?'

'I'm afraid it doesn't quite work that way,' Holly
forced herself to say firmly. 'Apart from the fact that
you should never take medication prescribed for someone else, different tablets cure different types of pain.
That's why you should always see a doctor if there's

something wrong with you. Different drugs suit different people. Specific conditions need specific treatment. Just because these sorted out your wife's problem and got rid of her headache, it doesn't mean they will do the same for your backache. Now, as you're here anyway, why don't you let me take a look and see if we can do something about it?'

Ten minutes later he trundled out of the consulting-room, not a happy man but appeased, and Holly turned to her next patient.

It was still raining when, having filed the last of her notes and finished her calls, she finally headed for the hospital to see Matt.

He looked better, happier, she was pleased to note as she walked into the ward and placed a pile of new magazines on the bed.

'I thought you might like some more light reading.' She bent to kiss him and he looked up, smiling.

'Holly, darling. You're the brightest thing that's happened to me all day.'

'How are you? You look better.'

'I *feel* better. They're even considering letting me go home.'

She frowned. 'Not too soon, I hope. It's early days yet. I know what you are. Once you're out of sight of the nurses you'll start doing things. . .'

He patted her hand. 'I've already been given a lecture. Besides——' he sobered '—I've learned my lesson. It's just that sitting here does nothing for my blood-pressure. Oh, they keep me on the move and I know exercise is good for me, but I'm bored. I shall feel happier among my own things.'

'I can understand that. I just worry about you.'

'I know——' he smiled '—and I worry about you. You look tired.'

'I am,' she sighed. 'It's been one of those days.'

'I gather Sam's had to go away for a while.'

'You know?'

'He mentioned that he had something to take care of.'

'So I gather,' she said briskly. 'I could do with a couple of days off myself. I don't suppose he happened to say what it was?'

'He didn't say and I didn't ask, but I'm sure Sam wouldn't have gone if it wasn't important.' He looked at her for a moment. 'Are you managing?'

'Yes, of course.' She gave him a smile, but it wasn't entirely true, she reflected later as she drove home. She missed Sam. Worse than that, she had discovered that she was jealous. How much did this girl still mean to him? He had said it was over, but how could that be true if she only had to call for Sam to drop everything and go running?

By morning the rain had turned to snow again and the waiting-room smelled of damp clothes and central heating. It was a relief to be kept busy. Market day brought people into town, and most seemed to like to kill two birds with one stone, collecting prescriptions or making appointments to visit the surgery at the same time. Holly couldn't blame them. Even so, her heart sank a little as she scanned the list.

'Give me a couple of minutes to make a few phone calls,' she said as Julie brought in the notes. 'By the way, how did you get on at the hospital?'

'Oh, fine. Well——' she gave a slight laugh '—I was so nervous, it was all a bit like a dream really. But it wasn't so bad at all. The specialist was very nice. He agrees with you, by the way. He doesn't think the lump is anything to worry about. But I'll soon get the results of the mammogram, hopefully in a couple of days.'

'I know it can't be easy for you.' Holly smiled

sympathetically. 'Are you sure you wouldn't like to take a few days off? I'm sure we could manage. . .'

'Oh, good heavens, no. I'd rather keep busy. The last thing I need is time to sit and brood. . .'

'I'm sure you've made a sensible decision. Look, it's a bit early yet, but later I could give the hospital a call, if you like, and try to pull a few strings. I'll see if they can let me know the results of the report, unofficially. It will depend, of course, on whether the consultant has had time to read the plates.'

'Oh, would you?'

'If that's what you want?'

Julie bit her lip, then nodded. 'I'd rather know one way or the other.'

'OK, leave it with me, then. I'll let you know as soon as I've managed to speak to someone.'

'I'm really grateful.'

'There's no need. That's what I'm here for. Besides, we have to look after our own, don't we?' For Julie's sake, she hoped the results were good. Being ninety-nine per cent sure about something was one thing, but it still left room for the tiny niggling doubt.

'Have you heard from Sam?'

'No.' Holly purposely kept her head lowered over the notes she was writing. 'But then I didn't expect to. Heavens, look at the time.' She pulled the pile of cards towards her, wishing Julie hadn't mentioned Sam. It had set off a train of thoughts she had been doing her best to avoid. Where was he? she wondered. What was he doing? Who was he with?

If nothing else, the past couple of days had given her the briefest insight into what it would be like not to have him around, and she didn't like what she saw. Professionally she knew she would survive, but on a personal level? In the past few weeks the edges of her reasoning seemed to have become blurred. Her life had been uncomplicated, all neatly mapped out. Now it was anything but. As far as Sam Stratton was concerned, out of sight was definitely not out of mind!

Two hours later she straightened, easing her aching shoulder-muscles. Finishing a letter she was writing to a local specialist, she sealed the envelope and reached for the phone. She was still speaking when Julie tapped at the door and poked her head round. Holly beckoned her in.

'Yes, Max. No, that's great news, I appreciate it.' She laughed.

From the door, Julie mouthed, 'I'll come back later,' but Holly motioned her to the chair.

'Nothing changes, does it? Still, keep up the good work. Love to Margaret and the children. Yes, we must do that. Bye.' Holly replaced the receiver.

'Sorry about that. I thought you'd finished.'

'Don't worry about it. I wanted to see you, anyway. I just managed to get hold of Max Preston.'

Julie's face paled a little. 'He's the consultant I saw.'

'Yes, that's right.' Holly reached forward to press the other girl's hand with her own. 'The results of your mammogram haven't been typed up yet, but he's taken a look at it and everything is fine. You've nothing to worry about. The lump is harmless—just a small fatty cyst.'

Tears suddenly welled in Julie's eyes. She brushed them away. 'Oh, thank God.' She reached for a hanky and blew her nose hard. 'I know you told me it was probably going to be all right, but. . .I feel as if a weight has been lifted off me.'

'Yes, I'm sure you do. It's perfectly understandable.'

'So what happens now?'

'Well, nothing—immediately anyway. Max feels that as the lump is very small and not causing any problems, it's best to leave it alone. If it starts to get bigger, or you feel unhappy about it, come and talk to me and I'll arrange another appointment for you to have the cyst aspirated. It's a perfectly simple procedure.' She hastened to offer the assurance. 'It simply means that a needle is inserted into the lump and the fluid is drawn off.' She smiled. 'A bit like an injection in reverse, or having a blood-test. The important thing is, you can stop worrying.'

'I wish I'd come to see you when I first found the lump.' Julie grinned as Holly closed her briefcase and followed her out to Reception. 'I could have saved myself weeks of needless worry, imagining the worst.'

'Fear is nearly always worse than the reality. I wish more people would come to see me when they have a problem. In so many cases we can prevent something that starts out as a simple problem becoming more serious.'

'Well, I shall certainly be spreading the word from now on.'

Perhaps it hadn't been such a bad day after all, Holly thought as she made her way out to the car.

It was late when finally she was able to head for home. By teatime it was already dark. The sky was clear and a smell of frost hung in the air.

She stirred restlessly. Suddenly the prospect of going back to the empty cottage seemed less than inviting, until she remembered that Sam was due back from London that evening.

Illogically her spirits rose until, having pulled up on the drive and switched off the engine, she discovered both cottages still in darkness and no sign of Sam's car.

Disappointment knotted her throat as she climbed out and let herself into the cottage, switching on the lights. She checked the answer-machine. There were no messages. Well, at least no news was good news.

Opening the door of the refrigerator, she found

herself staring blankly at the contents. What am I doing? she asked herself with a small sigh of disgust and swung it to a close. So he's late, so what? She felt exhausted as she bent to stir some life into the fire. 'So he needn't expect me to cover for him if he doesn't turn up,' she muttered furiously under her breath as she opened a can of soup, emptied the contents into a saucepan and waited for it to heat through. 'That's what.'

Carrying the improvised meal on a tray into the small sitting-room, she made a perfunctory attempt at eating while she watched the day's news on television.

Later, having showered and washed her hair, she had slipped into her nightie and a heavy towelling robe and was sitting huddled on the sofa, sipping at a cup of hot chocolate and stifling a yawn as she watched the late news. She willed the phone not to ring. The thought of having to get dressed again and turning out into the freezing night to answer an emergency call was almost too much to contemplate.

Reaching for her watch, she stared at the small dial. Eleven o'clock and still no sign of Sam. Perhaps he wasn't coming back, a tiny inner voice insisted, and was instantly banished. Don't be ridiculous. Of course he's coming back. He has to—if only to say goodbye.

Later she walked into the bedroom and stood in the darkness at the window, watching for the beam of the car's headlights. What if he had had an accident?

Tearing herself away, she climbed into bed and pulled the covers over her head. She wouldn't think about Sam. She wouldn't think about anything. But it wasn't that easy.

She sighed, tossing restlessly. Glancing at the clock, she lay with her arm flung across her eyes. She should be getting some sleep, she though irritably, not lying here trying to sort out her feelings, or lack of them, for Sam Stratton.

It was after midnight. With a stifled moan of impatience she flung back the covers, reached for her dressing-gown and padded, shivering, down to the kitchen to make herself a hot-water bottle and sit at the table, stifling her yawns.

Half an hour later a narrow beam of light edged its way between the gap in her bedroom curtains. Seconds later she heard the sound of a car on the gravel. The engine died, the lights went out. Sam was home. Worried? Who was worried? With a sigh she relaxed. Her eyes closed.

CHAPTER NINE

HOLLY woke suddenly to the loud shrilling of the telephone and stared disbelievingly at the clock, which now said just after five o'clock. She felt shaky and drugged as she fumbled for the receiver and said huskily, 'Dr Palmer.'

Minutes later she was struggling into her clothes and a sheepskin jacket as the kettle boiled and she gulped scalding black coffee to wake herself up. Her briefcase was ready on the hall table. Barely flicking a comb through her hair, she went out to the car, gasping as a wave of freezing air hit her.

The Croziers were a young family, living on one of the new estates that had sprung up in the past couple of years: Mum, Dad and two children—the youngest a baby of just over a year. Holly knew them all through their various visits to the surgery for treatment for routine childhood ailments, vaccinations and clinics. She knew Judy Crozier to be a sensible enough young woman, so if she phoned at five in the morning, sounding fairly agitated, there was likely to be a very good reason.

The door of the neat terraced house opened just as Holly reached it, her breath fanning white into the air.

'Oh, Doctor, thank heavens you're here. I'm so sorry to have to call you out. Come in.'

'I gather it's young Daniel.'

'That's right. He's through here.' Judy Crozier led the way into the neatly furnished sitting-room, where her husband, Mark, was sitting in front of the fire nursing a flushed and tearful infant on his knee. He shot a look of relief in Holly's direction and yawned widely.

'Sorry about that. We haven't had a lot of sleep.'

'He's been crying nearly all night. I thought he might be cutting some more teeth, but I've had a look and there's no sign. I gave him a dose of Calpol and it seemed to help for a while, but he's running a temperature, and you can see he's not right.'

Holly put her briefcase down, eased off her jacket and took the infant on to her knee. 'He's certainly not very happy, is he?'

'We tried to hang on until surgery opens, but we started getting really worried when he wouldn't stop crying, and he feels so hot.'

Holly reached for a thermometer, popping it into the child's armpit. 'Let's see just how bad it is and take a look at you while that cooks, shall we, young man?'

The infant strained away from her, rubbing tearfully at his eyes as she made a gentle examination for any swollen glands and managed, with difficulty, to peer into his mouth.

'Mmm, well, his throat's OK.' She retrieved the thermometer, frowning as she shook it down. 'But his temperature is certainly up.' She reached into her briefcase for her stethoscope. 'Has he been sick?'

'No.'

'And there's no sign of a rash. Let's just have a listen to your chest, shall we? Yes, well, that's clear.' She looked at the baby's flushed cheeks. 'So, we'll check your ears. I know.' She gave a slightly apologetic smile as she produced an autiscope and proceeded to examine his ears, under protest. 'Ah, that's the culprit. All right, little fellow, you can go back to your dad. He's got a nasty ear infection. The right one is not too bad but the left is quite badly inflamed. I'm not surprised he's unhappy. It's probably been building up for days. It's a good thing you called me. Ear infections can be nasty things—they're certainly not something you should ignore, especially in a small child.'

She took out a prescription pad. 'I'll write him up for a course of antibiotics. I'm afraid it's probably going to be twenty-four hours or so before they start to have any noticeable effect. In the meantime, though, you can give him the Calpol. At least it will help to bring his temperature down and should ease the pain.'

'We're ever so grateful.' Judy Crozier's anxieties were clearly alleviated, simply by knowing the cause of her baby's distress. 'Will you stay and have a cup of coffee?'

'I'd love one.' Why not?—Holly thought. There was no point in going back to the cottage and falling into bed and probably into a deep sleep, only to have to go through the whole process of having to climb out again.

Driving to the surgery half an hour later, as the first pale streaks of daylight were creeping into the sky, she had time to appreciate not only the beauty of the passing scenery, but also the peace and tranquillity of a time of day before the roads began to fill with traffic as people set about the business of the day.

Or indeed the business of the surgery, usually beginning with the first ringing of the telephone, and from then on continuing, seemingly without pause, until several hours later.

At least arriving early had its advantages, Holly thought as she dealt, uninterrupted, with a backlog of mail, an assortment of official forms still waiting to be filled in, and letters that were long overdue.

It came almost as something of a surprise when Julie popped her head round the door to say, 'Someone's eager this morning. What's this, then? Trying to put the rest of us to shame or something?'

'Nothing so noble.' Holly looked up, grinning. 'I was

called out at five o'clock.' She stifled a yawn. 'By the time I'd finished it was hardly worth going back to bed. So I thought I'd do some catching up.' She leaned back, stretching. 'And now I suppose you're going to tell me there's a room full of patients.'

''Fraid so.' Smilingly unrepentant, Julie placed the cards on the desk. 'Oh, and those blood-test results you wanted have come through. I put them on top of the pile.' She indicated the morning's mail.

'At last. Anything else of interest?'

'Mr Brinton phoned to ask for a repeat prescription of the anti-inflammatory tablets you gave him a couple of months ago. I checked his records and he's already had two lots, so I said you would need to see him before you could write another prescription.'

'Good girl. I know the tablets do the trick but I don't want to keep him on them longer than is absolutely necessary.' She said casually, 'Is Dr Stratton in yet?'

'Mmm, about ten minutes ago. He went straight through to his room. I expect he wants to make up for lost time.'

'Probably.' She made a play of tidying her desk. 'Talking of which, it's time I made a start. Oh, and these letters are for the post.'

Somehow she managed to get through the morning list. Most of the patients seemed to be suffering from fairly minor coughs and colds with all their varying symptoms, and she found herself wondering why they didn't simply take to their beds, or dose themselves with whatever favourite remedy suited them best, rather than coming to the surgery.

By the time she finally saw the last patient out and went gratefully in search of coffee, she took her own advice, and was just swallowing a couple of aspirins when the door opened and Sam stood there.

He was wearing a dark suit, he looked tired and cold,

and it needed an effort of will on her part not to go to him and put her arms around him.

'If that's coffee, I wouldn't mind some. Strong, black, three sugars.'

'You look awful.'

'Thanks.' His mouth twisted. 'I was late getting back last night. I hope I didn't disturb you?'

Not nearly as much as he was disturbing her now. She ran a shaky hand through her hair before turning to pour coffee—anything to keep herself occupied.

'Who, me? I slept like a log. Didn't hear a thing.' Mentally she crossed her fingers on the lie, handing him the mug and watching as he drank the scalding liquid gratefully.

'I'm sorry I had to ask you to cover for me.'

His height and presence in the small room were having a strange effect on her. He was standing only an arm's length away and she found herself wanting to reach out and touch him, to draw him closer.

'Forget it.' She managed a smile as she refilled her own cup. 'Just don't make a habit out of it, that's all.'

His glittering gaze was brooding. 'Dare I hope that you might have missed me, Holly?'

Her pulse-rate accelerated dangerously. She chose purposely to misunderstand him. 'Harry Bickerstaff was an experience I'd rather not repeat too often. He's all yours, thank you very much.'

'That wasn't quite what I had in mind,' he said huskily, moving closer, and she found her gaze drawn to the firm line of his jaw, the sensuous mouth and blue eyes which seemed to be having a strangely hypnotic effect, drawing her towards him.

His dark, expensively cut jacket brushed against her skin, sending dangerous signals to her brain.

'I—I shouldn't be here.' She had to clear her throat.

'I've a list of calls that could take all afternoon at this rate. I'll catch up with you later, maybe.'

'Holly?'

She hesitated at the door.

'I suppose it's too late to take you up on that offer of a meal?'

She closed her eyes briefly. Don't do this to me, Sam, she thought. Right now my resistance is too low. I can't play games. She stifled a sigh as she turned to face him, deciding that flippancy made the best defence.

'Last night's casserole may be a little the worse for wear.' She met his gaze and swallowed hard. I'm so weak, she thought. 'When did you have in mind? I'm taking a first-aid class tonight.'

'Day after tomorrow? I'll provide the wine. I'll even cook, if you absolutely insist.'

'Fine. I'll raid the freezer.'

She also shopped for steaks and salad and fresh fruit. A day off had its advantages, unless you preferred not to be alone with your thoughts and, right now, too much time to think was playing havoc with her nerves, Holly decided as she ran a hand in a small nervous gesture through her hair.

For some crazy reason she felt like a schoolgirl about to go on her first date, except that there was nothing even remotely childlike about her feelings for Sam.

Having showered, washed her hair and brushed the chestnut waves until they shone, she sat in front of the mirror to apply a light covering of make-up, and felt the nervousness she had been fighting all day well up with a new intensity. Just because Sam was back didn't mean he was here to stay, her inner voice warned. She couldn't imagine now what had possessed her to agree to have dinner with him, especially dinner alone, but it was too late to back out now.

She had decided to wear a plain but elegant fitted black skirt with a jade-coloured silk blouse. Gold clips in her ears added a touch of sparkle. Slipping her feet into slender-heeled shoes, she took a deep breath before collecting from the kitchen her mobile phone and the basket containing the food.

Sam opened the door the instant she reached it, almost as if he had been waiting for her knock. She hesitated in the doorway.

'I hope I'm not too early? I brought steaks and——' She broke off, aware of his penetrating gaze, raking her slowly from head to toe, lingering with disturbing intensity on the curve of her breasts, the narrowness of her waist emphasised by the skirt. Panic hit her. She stared down at herself, then at his own casual jeans and sweater, and passed her tongue over her dry lips. 'I wasn't sure what to wear.'

'You look beautiful,' Sam put in softly. 'You'd better come into the warm, it's freezing out there.' She stepped into the neatly furnished sitting-room. 'Make yourself at home. I'll take the food through to the kitchen. How do you like your steak?'

'Rare,' she called after him. Listening to the sounds coming from the kitchen, she took advantage of the moments alone to study the room, her eye caught by the details, subtle changes he had made even in so short a time, changes which stamped his own personality upon it—the dark wood furniture, a lamp reflected in polished surfaces, pictures on the walls, a log fire in the open hearth.

'I'll be with you in a minute. Why don't you pour some drinks?'

'I'm on call, don't forget,' she raised her voice to remind him.

'I keep trying. How about some orange juice?'

She spun round to see him standing in the doorway.

'Orange juice will be fine.' He came towards her and she accepted the proffered glass. 'Do you need any help out there?'

He shook his head. 'Everything is under control.'

Except my heart, she thought wildly. There was something disturbingly arousing about him as he stood with the firelight behind him, the faded jeans hugging his hips, his eyes appearing a deeper blue than ever.

She let her gaze fall warily. 'I'm not used to being waited on.'

'Why not just relax and enjoy it?'

She gave a slight laugh. 'I feel guilty.'

'In that case, come into the kitchen and supervise,' he said softly. He was leaning forward and she could smell the subtle, musky undertones of his aftershave. The effect of his nearness was creating an intensity of sexual awareness she had never known before. It was a heady, intoxicating sensation. 'We should do this more often.'

'I'm not sure that's a good idea,' she murmured breathlessly, tilting her head back to look up at him. For an instant she felt him tense, then he bent his head and the sensuous mouth swooped to take gentle possession of her lips. The effect was devastating. Suddenly resistance was a word that seemed to have been removed from her vocabulary as, without warning, his palm slid round her waist, drawing her towards him. His mouth was warm and firm and she was helpless to prevent the faint quivering of her lips beneath his as he caught her off-guard, unprepared for that sensual onslaught.

When, finally, he released her, it was to say huskily, 'I think we'd better eat, before I forget why you're here and things get well and truly out of hand.'

She whispered, 'I think I just lost my appetite for food.'

Laughter rumbled deep in his throat. 'I can think of worse ways to diet.' He brushed a hand against her cheek and sobered. 'I've no intention of rushing things, however much I might be tempted. Come on, let's eat. We can talk later.'

She told herself she wouldn't be able to eat a thing, but when it came to it she demolished the steak enthusiastically. Sam poured red wine.

'One small glass won't do any harm.'

Her head was already spinning, though not from the effects of any alcohol. In no time at all, it seemed, she had finished the lightest of fruit salads and sat back replete.

'That was marvellous. I must have been more hungry than I realised.'

Sam grinned. 'I like to see someone who enjoys their food. Come on.' He rose to his feet. 'I suppose brandy is out. I'll make some coffee later. Right now I don't think I can bear to let you go.'

She shook her head. 'No coffee for me. Can I help. . .?'

'Leave it,' he said huskily, drawing her to her feet, his gaze holding hers. His blue eyes searched her face intently as he touched her cheek. 'Why don't we just relax in front of the fire?'

The effect of his touch was even more potent than brandy could ever be. She drew a shuddering breath as his hand moved to caress her breast, shocked as the taut nipple flowered in instant response. She tilted her head back to look at him, her hands against his chest.

'I take it you managed to sort out the problem, whatever it was?'

A smile tugged at his mouth as he made a teasing foray against her lips and moved to her ears. 'Problem?'

'Sam, I'm trying to be serious. What about Lisa?'

'Lisa?' He frowned. 'What does Lisa have to do with any of this?'

Holly sighed. 'She must still mean something to you. She only had to call for you to drop everything and go running.' She tried to release herself gently from his grasp, but his hold merely tightened. 'It can't have been easy.'

His dark brows drew together.

'Going back never is. We lived together for three years. That's a long time to get to know someone, but I promise you——' his warm breath was against her hair '—there's nothing for you to worry about. Trust me, Holly.'

She wanted to, desperately.

A nerve pulsed in his jaw, then he drew her slowly towards him. He groaned softly as his mouth made teasing advances against her lips, her throat, the lobes of her ears and back to her unresisting mouth, claiming it with a determination that left them both breathless.

She responded with a ferocity that matched his own, driven by a raw kind of hunger. Sam raised his head briefly, breathing hard as he stroked her hair.

'I didn't intend rushing things,' he said huskily. 'I'm not sure I can stick to that. I want you, Holly.'

'I know.' She broke off as he kissed her again. She could feel the heat of his body through the fabric of his sweater. His hands had long since dealt with the buttons of her blouse and were moving over her body, rousing her to a peak of desperation. She closed her eyes, moaning softly as the whole gamut of emotions ran through her.

'I love you, Holly.'

'I know,' she sighed fretfully. 'I didn't intend for this to happen. . .'

He raised his head to look down at her with glittering eyes. 'I know you've been hurt. I can't promise to live forever. I *can* tell you that I'll always love you, care for you. Given the choice, I'd never want to leave you, but I'm human, Holly. I won't make promises I can't keep.'

'I loved Martin,' she said weakly.

'I know.' Sam's hand under her chin forced her to look at him. 'And I wouldn't want to change that. What you had together was special. But that doesn't mean that what we have can't be special too, maybe in a different way, but just as strong, just as important.'

He was right; she saw that now. She had tried to fight it, to tell herself that Martin was, would always be, the only man in her life, but it was no defence against this man who had forced her to see that she could love again.

The shock of the admission made her senses reel. She was in love with Sam. She raised herself to brush her lips against his mouth. 'I want you too. I—I love you too.'

He drew a harsh breath as he looked at her for a long moment, then pulled her roughly towards him. 'Stay with me tonight, Holly.'

His hands were moving over her body, rousing her again. She closed her eyes, moaning softly.

'This is completely crazy.'

'I know,' he breathed as he slid her blouse over her shoulders.

'I'm still on call,' she protested weakly. 'I need my sleep.'

'We can sleep later.'

She rocked on her feet, her senses seeming drugged as she looked up at him. 'People are bound to talk.'

'We haven't given them any reason—yet.' His fingers were at the waistband of her skirt.

The mobile phone rang. Involuntarily she stiffened.

'Ignore it,' he rasped.

'I can't.' She detached herself slowly from his arms.

Sam cursed under his breath, grinning as she fumbled to restore her blouse to order before reaching for the phone.

'Yes, Dr Palmer speaking.' She reached up to press her fingers against Sam's marauding lips. 'Yes, and he has a temperature? Right, I'll be there in about twenty minutes.' She struggled to her feet, raking a hand through her hair. 'I have to go, Sam.'

'I know.' He followed her to the door, helping her into her jacket, his hands tightening on her shoulders. 'I'll be here when you get back.'

'It may be late.'

'It doesn't matter.' He bent his head to kiss her. 'Just be as quick as you can, and take care.'

In the event, it was over a hour before Holly was finally able to head for home, tired but happy. The car's windscreen-wipers moved sluggishly under the weight of falling snow, heavy flakes drifting like moths out of the darkness.

Pulling up on the drive, she cut the ignition and smilingly reached for her briefcase. Sam hadn't drawn the curtains and the lights from his cottage were on, welcoming and warm. Her boots made soft squeaking noises as she hurried, head bent, through the snow.

Smiling, she raised her hand, but as she was about to tap against the window the sight of an unfamiliar car parked beneath the trees caused her to halt, frowning, in her tracks. It was a little late for visitors, surely? What should she do? Make her presence known, or come back later when whoever it was had gone?

As she hesitated a movement inside the cottage drew her attention. Standing in the darkness looking in, she saw Sam.

He wasn't alone. As she watched a young woman rose to her feet from the sofa, a glass in her hand as she reached up to run a hand through Sam's hair before his head came down and they kissed, oblivious to the figure gazing in at the window.

A wave of nausea threatened to engulf Holly. She couldn't believe it was happening. How could Sam *let* it happen when, little more than an hour ago, he had held her in his arms and said that he loved her?

Suddenly, everything became clear. This was the reason he had delayed making a decision about joining the partnership—because he was unsure about the future. Because, deep down, even if he didn't choose to admit it, he was still in love with Lisa. For Holly had no doubts that Lisa was the girl in Sam's arms.

Tears welled up in her eyes as, slowly, shocked, she backed away, a cold wash of despair running through her veins, and she shivered violently. How could she have been so naïve, ever have imagined that she really knew Sam?

Trust him, he had said, and she had done just that. She had let down her guard and he had betrayed her, but at least she had discovered the truth in time.

CHAPTER TEN

WHEN she climbed into bed later, Holly's numbed senses were gradually lulled into an exhausted sleep, to be punctuated by dreams in which someone slammed a succession of car doors before driving away. Except that it wasn't a dream. When finally she emerged from the cottage the following morning, the other car was gone, and so was Sam's.

Holly had woken with a splitting headache, and to the horrifying realisation that she had overslept. Maybe because she had her mind on other things, or simply because she had been tired, she had forgotten to set the alarm, and consequently arrived at the surgery ten minutes late, breathless, and having had no breakfast other than a hastily swallowed cup of coffee.

Any hopes she might have had of being able to avoid seeing Sam were dashed as he appeared just as she was at the reception desk, making her apologies to Julie and the waiting patients.

For a instant their eyes met and she experienced a brief sense of shock. He looked as if he had scarcely slept. Which, she told herself resignedly, might be true.

'Remind me to talk to Kate about seeing Mr Roberts for another blood-pressure check, will you?' she said to Julie, before turning away deliberately to study her list of calls with an attention it didn't warrant.

'Holly, wait.' Sam's hand came down on her arm. 'I need to talk to you.'

'I'm sorry, I'm busy. I don't have time.' She tried to side-step, but he was blocking her path, his face taut as he looked at her.

'You didn't come back last night. I waited.'

'No, it was late and I was tired. Besides——' she shuffled the bundle of cards '—you had a visitor. I didn't want to intrude. Now, if you'll excuse me, I really am busy. Julie?' She turned away. 'I don't seem to have Mrs Driscoll's notes. If you can rustle them up for me. . .I thought I'd pop in and see her later.'

Julie's glance flickered between the two of them. 'Right, I'll just get them for you.'

'Thanks. I'd better get started. At this rate I'll be lucky to get back from my calls before afternoon surgery.' She started to make her way along the corridor. Sam followed, his expression grim. 'Holly, at least let me explain. It isn't what you think.'

'You don't know what I'm thinking,' she said flatly. 'In any case, it makes no difference. I made a mistake. Fortunately I realised in time. Let's leave it at that, shall we?' She gave him a remote smile and turned away.

'Holly, please——'

'Oh, Dr Stratton, there's a call for you. . .' Julie's voice broke into the tension between them.

'Damn it, can't you take a message?'

'It's about some test results for Mr Walker. I thought you'd prefer to deal with it. . .'

He swore softly under his breath. 'Holly, we have to talk.'

But she was already walking away. If she talked to Sam, she would end up in his arms. Anger was the only defence she had left, and she was clinging to it as if her life depended on it.

Somehow she got through the morning. 'Right, Mrs Andrews.' She escorted the last of her patients to the door. 'I'd keep young Barry home from school for a couple of days, just until his temperature gets back to normal. Stick to the light diet and plenty of fluids, and

I'm sure he'll soon be feeling much better. If not, or if you're at all worried, give me a call or bring him back to see me.'

Returning to her room, she checked her diary, made a phone call, and then made her way to Reception. 'I'm off.' Handing over the cards, she glanced at her watch. 'If I hurry I might just manage to grab a quick sandwich before I start my calls.'

Julie glanced anxiously out of the window. 'Go carefully. It's looking a bit dodgy out there. I wouldn't be surprised if we're in for some more snow.'

Holly smiled. 'I make a point of carrying a spade in the boot. If the worst comes to the worst I'll dig myself out.'

'Don't joke,' Julie grinned. 'It's been known to happen.'

A door along the corridor opened and Sam emerged, grim-faced.

'Yes, well, I'll see you later.' By the time Holly had reached her car and was fumbling to get the key in the lock, Sam was beside her.

She cursed as the key refused to turn. Sam's hand came down over hers. 'Holly, we can't leave things like this. We have to talk.'

'There's nothing to talk about,' she reiterated flatly. From the moment Sam Stratton had walked into her life it had become full of complications. She felt as if she were walking on quicksand. The more she struggled to break free, it seemed, the deeper she was being sucked in.

'It isn't the way you think.'

She opened her eyes to fling a look in his direction. There was no mistaking the strain on his face. Her own emotions were so close to the surface that she wasn't sure she could trust herself to be near him without letting go, yet she felt the distance that had opened up between them as painfully as if it were tangible.

Never before had she been so starkly aware of her own vulnerability. For so long she had clung to her memories—felt, if not happy, at least safe, until Sam had come along, breaking down all her carefully erected barriers. Well, barriers could be rebuilt.

With an effort she turned the key in the lock. 'You couldn't possibly know what I think, Sam. In any case, it really doesn't matter.'

His mouth tightened. 'I can't believe you mean that. I won't believe it. Are you saying I misread the signals?'

'It seems we both did.' Colour heightened her cheeks as she wrenched open the car door and climbed in.

'At least talk to me, Holly.'

She sighed and wound down the window. 'I think it would be better if we kept to a strictly business relationship from now on. After all, that's what this was supposed to be. That way no one gets hurt.' But it was already too late for that, she thought as she drove away. As far as she was concerned, the damage was already done.

Back at the cottage, she drank a quick cup of coffee, then changed out of her skirt into a pair of black trousers and a sweater. Having persuaded Thomas to be brave and go outside, she checked the messages on her answer-machine. One more call to add to the list—at this rate she'd never make it back for surgery—and a message from Uncle Matt, to say that he was being allowed home in a couple of days. One piece of bright news in an otherwise fairly foul day, Holly thought as she made her way through a deepening layer of snow towards the car.

By mid-afternoon she had to switch on the headlights, and the temperature had plummeted by several degrees. Climbing out of her car, she locked the door and stood for a few seconds, breathing hard as she made the trek across the farmyard. The door was opened by an anxious-looking woman of about fifty.

'I'm sorry it took me a while to get to you, Mary,' Holly apologised as she stepped inside the big, stone-built house, brushing flakes of snow from her hair as she did so. 'I've a list of calls as long as your arm and this weather isn't helping.'

'Aye, and I reckon we're in for a good load more yet. Come in. Will you have a cup of tea? I've just made a fresh one for Dad.'

'I'd love to, Mary——' Holly glanced, frowning, at her watch '—but I'd better not.' She smiled ruefully. 'I smell scones, too.'

'There's a fresh batch just out of the oven. Maybe you'll take a few with you when you go?' Mary Clay had the weathered features of someone who had always worked the land. Her grandfather had been a farmer, as had her father, and she had married a farmer. Following his death in a tractor accident some ten years earlier, Mary's sons had helped out. They were a close-knit family and it had been taken for granted that, when her seventy-year-old father had a stroke and needed looking after, it would be Mary who would uncomplainingly assume the burden without ever thinking of it as such.

'How is your father, Mary?'

'Oh, he's not so bright this past couple of days.' Shedding her apron, Mary led the way towards the stairs. 'He had a bit of a sniffle last week.'

'You should have called me.'

'You know what he's like, can't abide fuss, but when he took to his bed I knew it was more serious. He's never been a man who liked his bed.' She pushed open the door. 'Hello, Dad. Here's Dr Palmer just popped in to see you.'

'Hello, Fred, how are you?'

The occupant of the bed raised one frail hand, turning his head to look in her direction.

'I gather you're feeling a bit poorly. Will you let me just check you over and listen to your chest? Perhaps we can make you feel a bit more comfortable.' With Mary supporting her father, Holly made a quick but thorough examination before removing her stethoscope and helping to lie him gently back against the pillows.

Moving slightly away from the bed, she said, 'I'm afraid he's definitely got a bit of an infection.'

'I suppose that means hospital?' Mary's face was troubled. 'He's not going to be happy about it.'

'No, I realise that, but I do think it would be best, Mary. The fact that he isn't mobile after his stroke isn't helping things. I really feel, for a few days at least, he needs the sort of care that with the best will in the world you can't give him here. I'd feel happier if the experts could keep an eye on him.'

'Aye, well, I'll talk to him and persuade him it's for the best.'

'I'll phone through for an ambulance.' Holly glanced out of the window. 'It may take a while, but at least we'll have him tucked up safe and sound by tonight.'

It was already dark when she returned to the practice, parked her car and ran through the gusting, snow-laden wind into the surgery. A peep at the crowded waiting-room and the expectant looks on the faces turned in her direction sent her hurrying through to Reception.

'What on earth's going on?' She looked pointedly at her watch. 'It's like rush-hour at Waterloo Station out there. Where's Sam, for heaven's sake? Half those patients are his.'

'I know, I'm sorry.' The phone rang. Frowning, Julie reached for it, cupping her hand over the receiver. 'Sam's not in yet.'

'Well, I can see that. Of all the days to choose to be late. . .'

'Sam's out on an emergency call,' Betty interjected quietly as she came through from the office.

'Emergency?' Holly felt her heart miss a beat. 'What sort of emergency?'

'We're not too sure yet. He called in on his mobile phone, about half an hour ago.' Betty placed a file of typed letters on the desk. 'Julie took the message.'

'Did he say where he was?'

Replacing the receiver, Julie scribbled a note before looking up. 'It was all a bit quick. He just said there'd been an accident on the Radleigh bypass, that he was on the scene, and to let you know he'd be late getting back for surgery.'

Holly swallowed hard on the sudden dryness in her throat. 'Did he say what sort of accident?'

'He said a pile-up.' Julie frowned apologetically. 'Several vehicles were involved, and there were casualties. That's all. He had to go.'

A tiny finger of fear stabbed at Holly's heart. Had Sam's been one of the vehicles involved? How else would he have been so close to the scene? He might be hurt.

Mentally she shook herself. This was ridiculous. Sam was a doctor, he was at the scene of an accident, he was doing his job. With an effort she fought to bring her feelings under control.

'Well, obviously we've got to come up with some contingency plan here,' she said briskly. 'Betty, will you have a word with the patients? Explain what's happened and if Sam isn't back in. . .half an hour, start shunting any urgent cases over to me. See if the rest would mind coming back tomorrow or, if that isn't possible, arrange a home visit.'

'You mean general reassurance and damage limitation?' Betty smiled.

Holly managed an answering grin. 'I couldn't have put it better. Right, I'd better make a start.' She gave a mock-groan as a bundle of cards was thrust into her hands. 'Where do they all come from?'

'Maybe they're all stocking up before they get snowed in,' Julie grinned.

'I can't say I blame them.' Holly gave a rueful smile and fled to her consulting-room, where she shed her jacket, glancing briefly out of the window. It was snowing even harder and Sam was out there. Suddenly she found herself wishing he would walk through the door, that he would be here, touchable, safe.

For the next hour and a half she worked steadily, sighing with relief as, finally, she saw her last patient to the door. 'Now, don't forget, no more DIY. Give that back of yours a rest, for the next couple of weeks at least, Mr Gibson. Come back and see me if you're still having problems.'

'A bit of a beggar, that. Shelves still need fixing.'

'Shelves can wait.'

'You tell our Edie that.'

Summoning a smile, Holly followed him along the corridor. Sam's door was closed. A peep into the waiting-room showed it to be reassuringly empty. He must be back, then. Irrationally, her spirits leapt as she closed the outer door and made her way to the office.

'Well, that wasn't so bad after all. It was nice of Sam to make it. What time did he finally get here?'

'Sam's not in yet.'

'Not. . .' Instinctively Holly's glance went to the clock. 'But. . .' She felt the blood draining from her face. 'It's been nearly three hours.'

'I spoke to the patients as you asked,' Betty interjected

quietly. 'There was nothing that desperately needed attention. In the circumstances pretty well everyone agreed to come back, apart from Mr Craddock, and I said you'd call out some time tomorrow.'

'That's fine.' She was finding it hard to concentrate. 'But what's happened to Sam? He can't still be at the scene. They must have cleared it by now. Why hasn't he at least rung in?'

Betty looked at Julie, then said quietly, 'We got a call from the local police station about ten minutes ago.' She fumbled on the desk for a piece of paper.

Holly turned slowly to face the older woman, fear becoming tangible, something to be held off as long as she didn't give a name to it. 'And?'

'Apparently things are a bit more complicated.' Betty looked at her.

Holly moistened her dry lips with her tongue. 'He said it was a multiple pile-up. How much more complicated can it be?' She felt her heart thud. 'Is it—is it Sam?' Please, God, don't let it be Sam. Don't take him away believing I don't care.

'According to the sergeant I spoke to, the accident was particularly nasty. Snow was making visibility bad—it was dark.' Betty cleared her throat. 'One of the cars collided with a chemical tanker.'

Holly took a steadying breath. 'Just. . .tell me about Sam. Was his car one of those involved?'

'It's all a bit confused but, as far as we know, he isn't badly hurt.'

Holly felt her stomach tighten. 'Not badly hurt.' It was a statement, not a question, as she looked at the other woman. 'Why is he still at the scene?'

Betty lowered her gaze. 'Apparently one of the casualties is still trapped. He's injured, and getting him out is being made more difficult because of a suspected leak from the tanker. Sam—Sam is with the man, giving what medical help he can until the emergency services can free him.'

'I'm going out there.' Holly was already heading for the door.

'Holly, wait. There's nothing you can do. . .'

'I can find Sam.' If it's not too late. Please, God, don't let it be too late.

'Holly, they won't let you. . .'

'I'd like to see them try to stop me.'

The drive to the site of the accident seemed interminable and was made worse by the fact that, even from a distance, she could see the flashing lights of police cars and the emergency-service vehicles. All traffic had been cleared from the bypass and the effect, the silence combined with the dark, was almost eerie.

Hastily rigged emergency floodlights were trained on to a trail of wreckage that had once been several cars. Parking on the slip-road, Holly grabbed the waterproof jacket she always kept in the car, and reached for her briefcase.

'I'm sorry, miss.' A policeman came towards her. 'I don't know how you got here but you'll have to move. There's been an accident.'

'I'm a doctor—Dr Palmer. We got a call at the surgery at Radleigh. My—my colleague, Dr Stratton, is here on site. How bad is it?'

'Pretty bloody, and I've seen some in my time.' The man shook his head. 'I'm Sergeant Fielder, Dave Fielder, by the way. In the circumstances I'm glad to see you, Doctor. We can do with all the help we can get.' He led her towards the emergency-service vehicles.

It was like the worst kind of nightmare, Holly thought. Far worse than anything she could have imagined. She picked her way over pieces of twisted metal, sucking in air as she slipped, and regretting it as the bitingly cold air wafted into her lungs like a knife. Dave Fielder's hand came under her arm, supporting her, and she was grateful.

'How many casualties?' she asked, breathing hard.

'Three fatalities so far. God knows how there weren't more. Ten injured, three critical.' His mouth twisted into a line of weary resignation. 'Two of those were kids. They'll be lucky if they make it.' As he spoke an ambulance set off, siren wailing, into the night. 'We've managed to shift most of the vehicles and get them towed away. Watch out for the hose.'

She found her feet sliding on a layer of foam, drew a breath, and coughed. 'My God, what is that?' She pressed a hand to her nose and mouth.

'Chemicals. A tanker slid across both lanes. One of the cars hit him sideways-on. We still haven't been able to get the driver out. We know he's hurt, but until we can move him there's no telling what the full extent of his injuries is. I know I wouldn't like to be in there. It's like sitting on a time-bomb.'

And somewhere, in the middle of all that, was Sam.

Holly stopped, gasping painfully for breath, trying to shield her face against the force of the wind as her horrified gaze took in the full horror of the scene.

'What about Dr Stratton? Was he actually involved in the crash?'

'One of the tail-enders luckily. He's got a slight head wound. By rights he should have gone to hospital but he insisted on staying with the chap in the car.'

'He'll probably be glad of some help. I brought some extra medical supplies with me. Can you get me in there?'

'It's not a good idea.' Dave Fielder looked at her. 'You do realise the whole thing could go up?'

'So why are you still here?' She flung him a wry look, then sobered. 'All the more reason to get them out as quickly as possible. Two of us might be able to do it more quickly.'

'I'll come with you.'

'It's probably better if you don't. We're going to need all the room we can get if there's any chance of getting him out alive.' She glanced up and smiled. 'But thanks for the offer.'

Carefully she managed to manoeuvre around the wreckage of one car, steadying herself on the buckled bodywork. Snow was coming down more thickly as, taking a torch from her pocket, she worked her way along the length of the skewed tanker, peering underneath it, all the time conscious of the acrid smell of chemicals.

She gasped involuntarily as she saw the small car wedged solidly beneath it. It must have spun out of control and twisted, making a sideways impact. The front passenger seat was crushed almost beyond recognition.

As Holly shone her torch in at the window her heart gave a momentary lurch when she saw Sam. He had eased himself forward from the back seat, over the gear lever, and was supporting the injured man's head. His face looked grey and haggard.

He drew a ragged breath as he looked at her for one long, disbelieving moment, and she told herself she must have imagined the flicker of relief she saw etched in his features as he rasped, 'What the hell are you playing at? Get the hell out of here—*now*.'

Carefully she tugged fragments of broken glass out of the window, edging herself closer. 'I thought you might need some help.'

'Well, you were wrong.' His jaw was rigid with tension, and she saw the thin trickle of blood seeping slowly from a wound in his forehead. Her eyes blurred with sudden tears. She blinked them away, knowing that now wasn't the time to get emotional. She had to keep a clear head.

'I'm not going anywhere, Sam,' she said quietly, easing aside the buckled door so that she could get closer to the injured man. 'How is he?'

'Bad,' came the terse response. 'Head injuries, internal and maybe spinal. God knows how he's still breathing. Where the hell is that rescue team?'

'They're all out there, Sam, doing the best they can. They have to clear away the rest of the wreckage to get to you.' An oxygen mask covered the injured man's face. She pressed her numbed fingers against his neck. He groaned softly. 'It's all right, I'm a doctor. Help is on the way—just try to relax.'

For the first time she was able to see his features clearly, and she felt her stomach tighten. He couldn't have been more than eighteen. His blond hair was matted with blood, his breathing was shallow and uneven. One look at his face told her that they were racing against time. If he didn't get help in the next fifteen minutes, she didn't think he was going to make it.

'Can I take over from you in there?'

Sam shook his head and used his shoulder to wipe a trickle of blood from his cheek. 'I don't want to risk moving him.'

In a lowered voice, she said, 'His pulse is getting weaker, Sam. Has he had any painkillers?'

'Morphine. I gave him the last injection about an hour ago.'

'I've got some in my bag.' Easing herself carefully in the confined space, she filled a hypodermic with morphine and administered the injection. 'Do we know his name?'

'It's Tony, Tony Blakely.'

As she shivered in the darkness, her hand found and

briefly held Sam's. For a few seconds his gaze held hers, then she broke away. 'OK, Tony, this will help to stop the pain. We're going to stay with you until we can get you out of here and on your way to hospital. It won't be long now.'

'Get out of here, Holly,' Sam's voice rasped.

'I told you, I'm staying.' She glanced up at him. 'What about you? You're hurt.'

'It's a scratch. I'll survive.'

She frowned. 'It's more than a scratch. Have you got a headache?'

For the first time, his mouth twisted in the semblance of a smile. 'What do you think?'

She eased herself carefully into the rear seat and looked at him, feeling the tears well up again. 'I think. . .' She swallowed hard on the lump in her throat. 'I think I can't let you out of my sight for five minutes without your going off and doing something crazy.'

His free hand reached out, his fingers twining with hers as he eased her towards him. Instinctively she squeezed his hand. 'Are you suggesting I need looking after?' The words came slowly, almost in a whisper.

She closed her eyes and blinked hard before giving a forced laugh. 'That sounds like a pretty full-time job to me.'

'We've got all the time in the world, Holly.'

Or maybe just the next five minutes. A bubble of panic welled up, giving an edge to her voice. 'No matter what happens, I want you to know that I love you, Sam. You were right, I've wasted a lot of time. We need to talk.'

'Oh, God. . .'

She froze. 'Sam, what. . .?' In horrified silence she followed his gaze, saw young Tony Blakely's head slump forward. In an instant she was out of the car, crouching beside the youth, her fingers feeling for a pulse. Fumbling in her briefcase, she found her stethoscope, pushed his clothing aside and applied it to his chest, willing herself to find a heartbeat, clinging to hope even though every instinct told her it was too late. She straightened up, shaking her head. 'He's gone.'

'Not *now*, for God's sake. Hang on just for a few more minutes. We'll get you out.'

'It's no good, Sam,' she said quietly, her hand over his arm. 'It's too late. You did what you could.' She was vaguely aware of figures moving around the car.

'OK, Doc, we'll soon have you out of there.' Geoff Pickering, the chief fire officer, peered in at the shattered window. 'We've cleared the rest of the debris. A few minutes and we'll have the young laddie out and on his way to hospital.'

Holly straightened up. She sighed, suddenly very weary. Her head was pounding. 'I'm afraid Tony couldn't wait.'

Geoff bent forward to stare at the slumped figure, and shook his head. 'Sometimes I hate this bloody job.'

Sam was on his feet, swaying, rubbing at his arm to restore the circulation. He looked awful. In the flashing blue lights his features looked haggard.

'We'll get you off to hospital, anyway, sir, get that head of yours seen to.'

'There's no need,' Sam's voice grated. 'It's a cut, that's all. I'll be fine.'

An ambulanceman hovered. 'It might be best, just as a precaution. . .'

Holly felt the muscles in Sam's arm tense. She said quickly, 'It's all right, I'm a doctor. I'll make sure he's all right.'

'Well, if you're sure?'

She nodded, taking Sam's arm, looking up at him.

'We're going home. Come on, Sam. There's nothing more you can do here.'

The drive back to the cottage seemed to take forever. Sam sat slumped in his seat, saying nothing. She could sense the tension in him.

Cutting the ignition, she tried to summon the energy to move, to get out of the car. Sam sat beside her, his eyes closed, making no attempt to do so.

'Come on, Sam. I'm going to make some coffee.'

He drew a breath and turned his head to look at her. 'It's late.'

'I need to unwind.' She fumbled with her keys. 'I don't know about you, but it's been a hell of a day, one way or another.'

He followed her into the sitting-room, and stood rubbing at his eyes. She poured two brandies.

'I thought you said coffee?'

'I don't know about you, Sam, but I need something a little stronger.' She looked at him and thought, Right now, I need to be in your arms. 'You'd better let me take a look at that cut,' she said aloud. It was a mistake; it meant she had to move closer. Her hand reached up and she was surprised to find that it was shaking. 'I don't think it's too bad. It needs cleaning up.' Suddenly her voice had an edge to it. She was feeling angry without really knowing why. She said briskly, 'How do you feel?'

'My head aches.'

'Well, what do you expect, if you will insist on playing the hero?' she snapped ungraciously. 'You were damn lucky, Sam, damn lucky. You do realise what could have happened. . .?' She broke off, suddenly shivering violently. Only now was she beginning to realise the full enormity of it all, how easily it could all have gone wrong. Taking several deep breaths, she half turned away, only to feel Sam's hands on her shoulders, preventing her.

'Holly, what's wrong?'

She couldn't believe he was asking the question. He had nearly died and he wanted to know what was wrong! She looked up, her face taut with strain, to find him watching her, his lips set in a hard, fierce line.

'Wrong? Nothing's wrong. Why should anything be wrong?'

His own breathing was ragged as he held her, his hand cupping her chin, forcing her to look into the compelling, blue eyes. 'It's over, Holly. It's all right.' His face was gaunt as she stared up at him, then, with a sob, she went into the safe refuge of his arms.

'Oh, Sam, I thought I'd lost you.'

He was speaking softly as he held her, his own throat tightening in painful spasms. 'It's all right. Everything's going to be all right,' his voice rasped.

'You could have been killed.' Her voice was muffled as he held her close. 'I thought——'

'Don't!' His fingers brushed against her mouth, silencing the words, then, before she knew what was happening, his mouth came down on hers, relentless, firm, demanding.

They clung together, Holly offering no resistance as his hands moved over her body. He raised his head briefly to look down at her. 'I need you,' he groaned softly as his mouth made feathering advances over her throat, chin, lips and eyes, then back to her mouth again, claiming it with a fierce possession that left them both breathless.

She responded with a ferocity that matched his own, filled with a need to be part of him, to hold him, keep him safe. She could feel the heat of his body through the thin sweatshirt he was wearing. His own hands moved jerkily in an attempt to remove her sweater. He swore softly as it seemed to create a barrier between them, until he finally made contact with the warm silkiness of her skin. 'I love you,' he rasped.

'I love you too,' she said brokenly.

Sam gazed wonderingly into her eyes, then, almost hesitantly, drew her within the circle of his arms again. 'I was afraid I must have dreamed it. When you suddenly appeared out there, I thought I was hallucinating. I'd been thinking about you, thinking what a hell of a waste it had all been——'

'Don't, Sam.' Gently she pressed her fingers against his mouth. 'I've been such a fool. I was the one who wasted so much time, I see that now.' She had to force herself to speak through the tightness in her throat. 'It's just that. . .I told myself this could never happen again, that I'd never feel this way about anyone. . .' Her voice broke. 'I realise Lisa will always be part of your life. . .'

A groan rose in his throat as he silenced her with a kiss, hungrily, before raising his head to look at her. 'Holly, you're wrong. I was telling you the truth when I said that anything between me and Lisa was over long before I left. We're friends, but that's all there is—all there will ever be.'

She stared at him, wanting to believe, but fear gave an edge to her voice. 'I see. So when she phoned you it was to say a belated goodbye. That's why you had to see her again?'

'She was unhappy,' he said softly, and when she would have protested, tried to break away, his grasp tightened, forcing her to look at him. 'Lisa was involved with someone else. I knew about it. It had started before I left. That was one of the reasons——' He broke off to look at her, his hand brushing against her cheek.

'Sam, you don't have to——'

'I want to tell you. You have a right to know.' He

frowned. 'Things weren't working out between us, we both knew that. The split, when it finally came, was almost a relief. The reason Lisa phoned me was because she had decided to sell the flat. When I left I told her it was hers to do with as she liked. I knew I'd never go back there. She needed me to sign some papers.'

Holly raised one eyebrow. 'She couldn't use the postal system?'

His mouth twisted. 'I'd left a few things behind. She needed them out of the way. It made sense for me to collect them and sign the papers at the same time.' He sighed, running a hand through his hair. 'When I arrived Lisa was out. By the time she got there I'd cleared my things and was ready to leave. She was upset and wanted to talk.' His voice roughened. 'I suppose my being there, our being together in the flat. . .'

'She wanted it to be like old times,' Holly said softly.

Sam frowned. 'I knew it couldn't work. Deep down, I'm sure Lisa knew that too. She just. . .'

'She needed a shoulder to cry on.'

He gave a slight smile. 'Something like that.'

'What did you do?'

He shrugged. 'There was nothing I could do. We were going round in circles, talking, arguing, back to where we were. I left, spent the night with some friends. The next day I took care of a few things I had to do and came back here.'

'But. . .she followed you.' Holly looked at him uncertainly.

'That wasn't planned. I didn't know she was going to turn up, out of the blue.'

Holly frowned. 'She must still be hurting, Sam.' She looked up at him. 'I want to believe you when you say it's over, but. . .' She drew a deep breath. 'I saw you kiss her.'

His mouth tightened. 'What you saw was Lisa kissing *me*. She'd managed to convince herself that, if we talked, things would be all right, that somehow we could go back to where we were.' A nerve pulsed in his jaw. 'She was unhappy, and I suppose I felt guilty, even though it was crazy. I felt. . .responsible. She'd been part of my life for three years.'

'Poor Sam,' she murmured. 'And I didn't give you a chance to explain. What did you do?'

'What could I do? I let her talk. She had a good cry. It seems she and Richard weren't getting on so well.'

'Richard?'

'He's a director at the gallery where she works. I think she panicked. Our relationship had broken up, things suddenly weren't going right with Richard. . .'

'So better the devil you know?' Holly said, a hint of laughter in her voice as she reached up to brush a strand of hair from his eyes.

He made a soft growling noise as he caught her hand, imprisoning it in his. 'You're not taking this seriously, woman.'

'Oh, Sam.' Laughter bubbled up. 'I've taken it far too seriously for far too long. I suppose you know you're too soft for your own good? So what happened?'

He gave a short laugh. 'We talked, and talked some more. I gave her a few drinks and made lots of coffee. I finally persuaded her to phone Richard. They talked for an hour while I tried to make myself scarce—which isn't easy, I might add, in a small cottage. I imagine they sorted things out. Lisa was certainly bubbling afterwards. It was all down to some lovers' tiff.'

He bent his head to brush his lips against hers and looked at her, his eyes glittering. 'She spent the night in my bed—*alone*,' he added, grinning as her eyes widened. 'I could hardly throw her out into the night, could I?'

'Oh, no, Sam. Not you, not my knight in shining armour.'

'So, I spent the night on the couch, and in the morning Lisa went back to London. And that's all there was to it.'

Holly raised herself to kiss his nose. 'I believe you.' She tilted her head back and saw his eyes narrow.

'So what now?'

'When Uncle Matt asked you to stay, you said you had to think about it.' Holly frowned. 'You had doubts.'

He kissed her again and this time it was more demanding. 'I wasn't sure I had any reason to stay,' he said huskily. 'Ask me to stay, Holly.'

'Please stay, Sam.' She smiled up at him dreamily.

'Ask me nicely.'

'*Please* stay, Sam,' Holly murmured.

'I'll think about it.'

She hit him. He drew her roughly towards him and kissed her until they broke apart, breathlessly, and he looked at her with laughter in his eyes.

'You're sure now?'

'Sam, I've never been more sure of anything in my life. I think it would make everything. . .just perfect.'

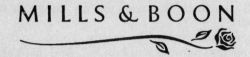

MILLS & BOON

LOVE ON CALL

The books for enjoyment this month are:

IMPOSSIBLE SECRET	Margaret Barker
A PRACTICE MADE PERFECT	Jean Evans
WEDDING SONG	Rebecca Lang
THE DECIDING FACTOR	Laura MacDonald

Treats in store!

Watch next month for the following absorbing stories:

LOVE WITHOUT MEASURE	Caroline Anderson
VERSATILE VET	Mary Bowring
TARRANT'S PRACTICE	Abigail Gordon
DOCTOR'S HONOUR	Marion Lennox

SPRING FLOWERS COMPETITION

How would you like a years supply of Temptation books ABSOLUTELY FREE? Well, you can win them all! All you have to do is complete the word puzzle below and send it in to us by 31st December 1995. The first 5 correct entries picked out of the bag after that date will win a years supply of Temptation books (*four books every month - worth over £90*). What could be easier?

COWSLIP
BLUEBELL
PRIMROSE
DAFFODIL
ANEMONE
DAISY
GORSE
TULIP
HONESTY
THRIFT

L	L	E	B	E	U	L	B	Q
P	R	I	M	R	O	S	E	A
I	D	O	D	Y	U	I	P	R
L	O	X	G	O	R	S	E	Y
S	T	H	R	I	F	T	M	S
W	P	I	L	U	T	F	K	I
O	E	N	O	M	E	N	A	A
C	H	O	N	E	S	T	Y	D

PLEASE TURN OVER FOR DETAILS OF HOW TO ENTER

HOW TO ENTER

Hidden in the grid are various British flowers that bloom in the Spring. You'll find the list next to the word puzzle overleaf and they can be read backwards, forwards, up, down, or diagonally. When you find a word, circle it or put a line through it.

After you have completed your word search, don't forget to fill in your name and address in the space provided and pop this page in an envelope (you don't need a stamp) and post it today. Hurry - competition ends 31st December 1995.

Mills & Boon Spring Flower Competition,
FREEPOST,
P.O. Box 344,
Croydon,
Surrey. CR9 9EL

Are you a Reader Service Subscriber?   Yes ❑   No ❑

Ms/Mrs/Miss/Mr _____

Address _____

_____

_____ Postcode _____

One application per household.   F

You may be mailed with other offers from other reputable companies as a result of this application. If you would prefer not to receive such offers, please tick box. ❑